Only Love

Only Love

SUSAN SALLIS

Harper & Row, Publishers

Only Love

Copyright © 1980 by Susan Diana Sallis

Library of Congress Cataloging in Publication Data
Sallis, Susan.
  Only love.

  SUMMARY: When she finds herself the object of a
young man's love, a spirited, physically handicapped
16-year-old is both touched and frightened for she knows
she may now have to share her painful secret.
  [1. Physically handicapped—Fiction] I. Title.
PZ7.S1533On 1980   [Fic]   79-2686
ISBN 0-06-025174-3
ISBN 0-06-025175-1 (lib. bdg.)

First Edition

To my family with all my love

1

 AS SOON AS I GOT to Thornton
Hall I knew it was going to be different. For one thing
it was a proper home—built by Sir Richard Thornton
for his enormous family way back in seventeen-some-
thing—and it had smashing gardens and its own
chapel and a reedy lake, besides a 1972 swimming
pool and a modern block with all modern conven-
iences. The whole atmosphere of the place was in-
triguing. Exciting. I decided to forget all past
botch-ups and really get stuck in here.

I arrived one early evening in June, met the boss
man, Douglas Beamish, Fellow of the Royal College
of Surgeons, and politely refused his offer of formal
introductions all around. He looked warmly serious
and used his favorite word: "You'd prefer to integrate

slowly?" And I came back, "Infiltrate I think. Yes, I'll infiltrate." He liked that and almost smiled.

Anyway the very next day I inherited this married couple from a girl who was at Thornton Hall before me and died. This couple—the Parrishes—couldn't have any children, apparently, so they joined the Friends of Thornton Hall and took an interest in one boy and one girl. Straight off they wanted me to call them Aunt Nell and Uncle Roger. I'd never had a pair of Friends of my own before, so I didn't think it would be too difficult, especially when I could stop them treating me as if I was six and slightly mental.

"Now Frances dear"—did her soft, breaking voice ever call me anything but Frances dear? I don't remember—"we can never be parents to you, of course. But we'd like to be more than ordinary aunt and uncle. We'd like to be friends. You'll have lots, of course. But we'd like to be *special*. People you can talk to—confide in . . ."

"Friends," I confirmed, nodding encouragingly.

She looked pleased and surprised. "Yes. Friends."

I met Uncle Roger's wishy-washy gray eyes and wondered if there was a laugh somewhere down there. There certainly wasn't in Aunt Nell's wide-open blue ones. She was so eager. That was the trouble with a lot of the female Friends. They wanted to help so much they were like a lot of horses straining baretoothed at their bits. And behind it all was the sharpest goad of all. Guilt. Because their body parts were all in running order; which was more than you could say for most of us here.

So I said, "Fine. Just fine." And in case they hadn't got the message, "That's okay by me."

We'd established that they were Friends *and* friends and Aunt Nell relaxed a bit. She was wearing a powder-blue sweater, supposed to match her eyes perhaps, and it emphasized her heavy breasts and red neck. Uncle Roger wore a tweed sports coat, gray flannels and a white shirt. I almost never saw him in anything but a white shirt.

He picked up the ball by producing a bag of sweets, offering me one and saying, "Good . . . well, as one friend to two others—what d'you think of Thornton Hall?"

Aunt Nell laughed on cue, and I grinned again obediently. It was so obvious they'd rehearsed at home beforehand.

"Smashing." I looked at the sweets. "I'm not supposed to. Extra weight, you know."

"Just this once." They looked roguish and conspiratorial. Then spoiled it all. "We asked Doctor Beamish."

"Thanks all the same." I shook my head. "We get enormous meals here." People always want to hear what you eat as if you were some unusual animal, so I gave them a menu. "We had soup for lunch—tomato, my favorite. Then pigs in blankets. Then apple charlotte with ice cream."

"Sounds nice." Uncle Roger glanced at Aunt Nell, passing the ball to her.

She said, "And your room, Frances dear—are you happy with your room?"

"Yes, thanks. It's a very interesting room. A funny shape—the window sticks out from the roof so there's a bit by the bed, then another bit around the corner."

"You don't have to thank us, dear. We're on your side, remember?" Aunt Nell tried to twinkle, but her eyes were too wide open. "I expect you mean a dormer window. Those rooms are on the second floor, Frances dear. Are you sure you can manage? Er— the wheelchair—"

I said quickly before she could get embarrassed, "Sure. There's a lift. Plenty of ramps."

I could have asked them up, but I'd only moved in yesterday and it was still not quite mine. I didn't want invaders yet. I'd already told the boss man I would clean it myself, and I'd put some Scotch tape across the door when I came down so that I'd know if anyone had been in.

Aunt Nell glanced at Uncle Roger and their eyes almost watered. "Well done, lass," said Uncle Roger.

Aunt Nell smiled. "We're proud of you already, d'you know that?"

This because I could use a lift? I shuffled about and tried to blush and tried not to shout, "Bullshit! Let's get on with it, get it over, so that I can explore and meet the others!" And there was a long deep silence.

Then Uncle Roger cleared his throat and said briskly, "Well now. We've covered the place—the food and your room. What about the people here?"

Thank God he didn't say patients. Or even residents. People covered the staff as well as us, and I always found the staff interesting.

4

I said experimentally, "Casey's okay. Nice legs. She's got her eye on Beamish, I think."

Aunt Nell's eyebrows went up and down in bewilderment. Uncle Roger at last managed a proper grin.

"You mean Staff Nurse Casey? She's certainly gorgeous, but Doctor Beamish is a dedicated man."

"So what? He's got eyes. She'll make him see her one of these days."

Aunt Nell's voice almost shredded away. "Frances dear. Really. I don't think you should talk like that about the staff."

Uncle Roger squeezed her powder-blue arm. "Why not? It shows our lass takes an interest in things outside herself. She's a sharp one—only been here a day and—"

". . . not the sort of thing one would wish her to . . ." Aunt Nell's protest petered out like surf in the shallows and she leaned forward again, determined to take me seriously. "Besides, Frances dear, don't you find that kind of—er—enameled prettiness—er—rather *hard?*"

I nodded, thrilled that she'd actually looked at someone and formed an opinion.

"She's tough, is Casey. That's what I like about her. She isn't going to let it get her down. Plenty of pancake and eye shadow and a few choice words . . ." She hadn't got a bedside manner. When I'd started yapping at her last night asking her questions, she'd told me to shut up and get to bed and I'd find out for myself in good time. I liked that because it was what she'd say to anyone whether they were paraplegic or not.

5

Uncle Roger entered into the spirit of the conversation pursing his lips judiciously. "Not the type for Doc Beamish, would you say, lass?"

I nodded again. "He needs someone like her. A protector. He's all quivery inside. Too sorry for us." I looked away from them both, hoping they wouldn't think I was being personal. My eyes met those of one of the old girls. Thornton Hall was like that; it contained young, old, middle-aged, everyone jumbled up just like in real life. There was even a pair of mentally deficient dogs. At least they acted mentally deficient, what with drooling and flopping about all over the place and thinking the old men's walking sticks were tree trunks. This old girl must have just had new teeth fitted, because she had a grin like a Jap officer in an old American war movie and as I looked at her she put up a quick hand and whipped out the top set. Then she gave an ecstatic sigh, smiled at me nicely, her chin jutting forward like a prizefighter's, and closed her eyes. I grinned.

Aunt Nell's hand fluttered about my arm again.

"No one could accuse you of that, Frances dear. Self-pity is obviously not one of your sins."

Again I wanted to shout, "Shit!" at the top of my voice. How long would it be before Uncle Roger and Aunt Nell realized I was no saint? I looked her straight in the eye.

"Don't be too sure of that. Beamish's raw compassion makes it difficult for him to see *any* woman. Which makes me damned sorry for myself. I think I could fancy him."

That did it. The blue eyes nearly fell out and the facial muscles would have snapped if they'd stretched any further.

"Frances. *Dear!* You really must not talk like that!"

"Why not? Because I've got no feelings from the waist down?"

She was even more appalled. "You know I didn't mean . . . You're only six*teen!*"

"Two years older than Juliet, I believe."

"It's not—" The voice snapped off and began again with difficulty. "I don't mean—" She reached for Uncle Roger and they shook together. "It was the *way* you . . . Frances dear, you sounded almost *coarse!*"

Uncle Roger's shaking was nothing to do with outrage. He was laughing. I realized it as Aunt Nell said that Victorian word—coarse. It was a chink of light in a dimming room.

"That's part of my trouble," I said solemnly. "I am coarse. It's got something to do with always wetting my knickers, I think. I dwell on the more basic things of life. Actually my feelings for Doctor Beamish would probably be very delicate. Yes, very delicate and proper, all things considered." I glanced meaningly at my useless thighs and then at Uncle Roger. But he wasn't laughing anymore. He had that raw look of agonized pity, and I wanted to remind him coldly that he hadn't got any kids so maybe he wasn't too hot in that way either. But I didn't. "It's so difficult to know how to put it . . . other than saying I could fancy Doc Beamish myself."

Aunt Nell sat up straight and smiled forgivingly.

7

But she obviously thought sex wasn't a suitable subject for a sixteen-year-old paraplegic, because she then said brightly, "Have you seen the games room? We understand you're very good at table tennis and billiards?"

I shook my head. "I've not seen anything much. Last night the interview with Beamish. Then up to my room. This morning—bath—examination—lunch—you."

"Let's take you along then, shall we?" Aunt Nell jumped up gratefully. "It'll be fun showing you around." She tried to get behind me and I turned my chair to face her. We were like boxers circling each other.

"Don't push me!" I heard my voice going up a notch and brought it down. "I can manage. I don't like to be pushed, thanks."

Aunt Nell fell back frustrated. Uncle Roger said easily, "That's good. It means we can go on talking without shouting over your shoulder."

There was more to Uncle Roger than met the eye. He pointed to double swing doors beyond the old girl with the teeth—sorry, without the teeth—and paced beside me. He was very tall, but he bent his head courteously, his hands clasped behind his back. If we'd had anything to say we could have talked without difficulty. As I maneuvered past the group of armchairs I spotted the teeth lying glisteningly on a side table. Without a thought I swept them into my tidy bag, which hung from the arm of my chair, and bowled myself straight at the doors so that they opened and immediately closed behind me. The old girl didn't see a thing. I wondered about a career in crime; who would suspect a thief in a wheelchair?

The games room was empty so soon after lunch. It was vast. The two billiard tables and three table tennis decks were lower than usual; there was a punching bag, dart boards, quoits, even a basketball court. Breathtaking.

Uncle Roger and Aunt Nell joined me, breathing audibly.

"It's marvelous," I said quickly. I spun my chair around the nearest table. "Better than anything I've seen before. Yes, it's quite a place, Thornton Hall. I'm going to like it."

Uncle Roger said, "You're expert in that." He nodded at my wheels and the indulgent tone had gone from his voice. "Anyone would have thought you wanted to get away from us."

Aunt Nell started before he'd finished. "Frances dear, what's happening? Why did you—?"

"I'm showing off." I laughed at them and went into reverse, spun onto the basketball court, did a figure eight. "I am good, aren't I?" I kept giggling and twisting around and Aunt Nell kept starting to say something and Uncle Roger restrained her with his hand on her arm. At last I had to stop before my arms dropped off. "Some girls get biceps like wrestlers," I panted, resting my hands on my knees. "I'm just lucky." I was proud of my arms and hands. I was wearing a tight black T-shirt with long sleeves that afternoon, and I'd done my nails a silvery pink. I could

9

see Aunt Nell was of two minds as to whether she should be pleased I took an interest in my appearance or whether she should disapprove of anyone physically handicapped being vain enough to use nail polish.

Anyway, Uncle Roger was still holding her back and as I sat there displaying my weary hands, he said calmly, "Frances. Why did you take Mrs. Gorman's dental plate just now?"

So I hadn't been completely invisible. Oh well, I fluttered my fingers and gasped a laugh, all feminine.

"I do things like that. I don't know why. They were there."

Aunt Nell was bewildered, out of her depth. The other girl—the one who died—was probably sad and submissive, and Aunt Nell thought I'd be the same. Uncle Roger gave me a long stare, then went to the corner and fetched a couple of folding chairs, opened them up and urged his wife to sit down.

He said, "What are you going to do with the teeth?"

"Put them back." I stared back at him. His neutral gray eyes held depths that I couldn't fathom but that gave me hope. I stopped being girlish and leaned forward slightly. "Don't you see? I like things to happen. Not just physiotherapy and playing table tennis and people dying. Things that *I* make happen. Nothing to do with the homes and hospitals. For instance"—it had only just occurred to me but it became a shining certainty on the instant—"before I leave Thornton Hall I'm going to fix things between Nurse Casey and Doc Beamish!"

They both recoiled as if from a gust of wind. Aunt

Nell's mouth opened slightly, but still she was speechless. Uncle Roger was the first to recover, and he started to grin again.

"I see. Should be interesting." He glanced at Aunt Nell, asking for her support. She made an obvious effort to relax. He went on, giving her time. "Somehow, Frances, the way you spoke of leaving here gave the impression you thought your stay might be short." He raised sandy brows at me humorously. That meant they didn't know. I'd made a point before I accepted the place here that no one must know. Beamish of course. But no one else. It didn't bother me much, but it bothered everyone else like hell. They thought because my days were numbered that they had to wear kid gloves and a halo when they were with me. I was grateful Beamish had kept his promise as far as Aunt Nell and Uncle Roger went—for their sakes. I couldn't imagine how they would manage otherwise.

"Could be." I grinned at them both and was glad to see Aunt Nell's still-parted lips tremble a slight response. "I get moved on quite a bit. No one liked my record player at the last place. The one before objected to my pets."

"Pets?" Aunt Nell was on my side now. I'd noticed how she fussed around the pair of mentally deficient dogs.

"Mice. I let them out of their cage for exercise. You should have seen how the staff jumped about."

"But you were only a little girl then. Surely a prank like that . . ."

I shrugged. "There were other things."

Aunt Nell's imagination boggled and she sat back

11

in her chair. Uncle Roger said rallyingly, "Well. No one will hear your player if you're up in the dormer room. And you've got the dogs—they'll be pets enough for you, I should think."

I grinned again. "If you could have seen them at lunchtime—I'm surprised they let them within a mile of the place."

"There you are. Thornton Hall is different. They'll probably put up with you."

I began to like him. We laughed and after a bit Aunt Nell joined in. Then I said I'd give Mrs. Gorman's teeth back and they trailed after me into the lounge. And there was poor old Mrs. Gorman going through her tidy bag like a maniac while one of the nurses stood over her and all her neighbors gazed on with interest.

The nurse walked off in disgust as I arrived.

"I've got them!" I slewed my chair around in front of the old lady and began to search my bag. "I'm sorry, Mrs. Gorman—I thought you'd be asleep for ages and I just—I just—" It sounded so feeble now that I couldn't go on.

I produced them and looked up, expecting her to be all to pieces like so many old people. But she had that toothless grin on her face again and her chin jutted toward me confidentially.

"You keep 'em, my love. Go on, put 'em back in that bag of yours! I hate the bleeding things and they'll only go on and on—'Persevere with them, Mrs. Gorman'—'You look years younger, Mrs. Gorman'!" She made a hissing sound of disgust. "As if I want to

12

look young and silly again! As if I can't mangle my food around quite well without them—and speak clearer, I'll be bound!" She closed her eye at me. "No. You did me a good turn, young lady. You keep them safe for me. If I want 'em, I'll know where to come."

I looked at her with my eyes popping to beat Aunt Nell's. It was like meeting an old friend; someone who enjoyed stirring things up as much as I did myself.

Uncle Roger leaned over me, his smile fully fledged. "The biter bit, eh Frances Adamson?"

I transferred my pop eyes to him and then to the gleaming, hideous false teeth in my hand. I began to laugh. Uncle Roger laughed. Mrs. Gorman cackled. Aunt Nell looked bewildered but willing to be amused. Another old girl and two men rustled newspapers disapprovingly. The dogs lolloped over and lay on their backs showing everything they'd got and smiling their mentally deficient smiles. A wheelchair and two buffer stools appeared from the terrace containing the usual assortment of misshapen bodies. The place was practically in an uproar.

A questing nurse arrived, and with a quick motion Mrs. Gorman whipped the teeth from my fingers and dropped them back into my tidy bag. At last Aunt Nell giggled.

"Listen," Uncle Roger said, crouching by the chair. "Don't do anything too drastic, will you? It would be nice if you could hang on here for a while."

I could have wept. Except that I never did.

13

2

 THE SCOTCH TAPE WAS unbroken on my door. I swung it open and sat still, staring at my room from the threshold. It had terrific possibilities. There's a lot to be said for functional homes, but their big drawback is that the architects have used up all the possibilities themselves. Thornton Hall might have been very functional for Sir Richard Thornton and his hordes of family and servants, but for physically handicapped people it was very nonfunctional. Which gave it terrific possibilities.

I left the door open and glided slowly into the tented glass of the dormer window. It was quite a big area, probably five by five, and the window came down low enough for me to see over the grounds to the new Avon bridge and the teeming motorway traffic. Directly below, the primrose-yellow plastic that covered the swimming pool glinted in the setting sun, and beyond that were trees and paths and more trees around a reedy lake. Loads of it, stretching right and left. I marked various things I'd like to see as soon as possible. I was determined to explore thoroughly; make it mine.

First there was the room. That must be welded to me first of all, so that even if I died tomorrow it would be Fran's room. Even if my mother had cared little enough to put me on the steps of the Social Security offices in Bristol without a name or pedigree or legs that worked, I was still a person. I didn't intend to go out like a guttering candle; people were going to know I'd been here. Me: Frances Adamson.

I turned slowly on my left wheel, surveying the low sloping ceiling that begged for posters, the pitted but glossy floorboard that might even be prized up to reveal secret caches. My trunk stood before the low cupboard, half unpacked. Dorothy, my black rag cat lying on top of forty pairs of knickers, my lacey half-cup bras still in their cellophane bags. As long as Dorothy had air and vision, the unpacking could wait until the morning, but I had to make a start on personalizing the room before dinner. The matter was of sudden, vital importance, and I usually fostered this sense of urgency that visited me periodically just in case it was foretelling a sudden end. Uncle Roger— maybe Aunt Nell—wanted me to stick around and, as I said, I didn't want to sink without trace like their other girl. So . . . so what?

15

The door blew a little farther open and said *Zeek*. A pleasant, nudging comment, reminding me of its solid wooden presence. I smiled at it, complimenting it for not being "faced up" like other less noble doors. It would take thumbtacks securely and with equanimity. The door *zeek*ed again and my smile broadened, because of course it was telling me to start right there; to blazon my presence on its glowing torso. But how? Not with the usual miscellany of pop posters. Something special. I rummaged through my magazines; brochures of Canada, rail trips in Scotland, a guide to London. At last I came upon the right thing just as the dinner gong shuddered along the passage. A nosegay of flowers so intensely blue they would make Aunt Nell's eyes look albino. I cut them out carefully and stuck them on temporarily with some of that putty stuff, closed the door, resealed it and studied the effect. Yes, it would do. Nothing but flower pictures would go on my door. I would call my room the flower room and make sure that the smell of flowers drowned even the deodorant which was supposed to cover my wet knickers.

I grinned with satisfaction as I spun toward the lift. And it was only as I pressed the ground-floor button that I realized those blue flowers were forget-me-nots. Appropriate of course, but a bit like a plea? I nearly went back and ripped them off. Then I thought if I hadn't recognized them instantly, neither would anyone else. And when they did they wouldn't connect a thing. Most people who worked in homes were undersensitive. They had to be, else they got raw like Doc Beamish; then they had to leave to protect themselves. That got me wondering how long I had to work on the Doc Beamish–Staff Nurse Casey romance, and that got the urgency syndrome started up again so I was practically fizzing as I waited for the lift doors to open and bowled myself down the ramp into the dining room. And of course I was last.

About a dozen pairs of eyes turned to me, most of them friendly, some of them tending to hostility. For a new girl I wasn't subdued enough. One of the helpers indicated the place I'd had at lunchtime: a round table for three with two thalidomide girls, younger than me and marvelously dexterous. But armless. And how could I be proud of my arms when they had none? The old guilt thing again.

I kept my beaming smile intact and swiveled around to Granny Gorman's side. There was no place laid but just enough room for my wheels. The old man on my left clicked with annoyance and snatched his tripod walking stick to the other side of him as if he thought I was after it. Granny didn't even notice my arrival and continued spooning soup into her toothless face with great concentration.

The helper galloped over.

"Dearie, your seat is over here. With Stella and Penny. Don't you remember?" Her voice was gay, indulgent, patronizing.

I twisted my head comically. Meant to be comically anyway.

"Funny, I could have sworn my seat's right here." I looked up at her winningly. Meant to be winningly anyway. "D'you think you could bring the old eating irons over here tonight? I have to sit next to Mrs. Gorman. For a special reason."

"Now dear, don't be difficult. Mrs. Gorman always sits next to Mr. Pope. She doesn't like change—older people don't, do they? So shall we just move across to—"

I hung on to my wheels grimly while she tugged from the back.

"Mrs. Gorman can't do without me tonight though, can you Mrs. Gorman?" I almost yelled into her ear. "You might need me, mightn't you, Mrs. Gorman?"

"Eh?" The tortoise head turned toward me with difficulty. "Oh it's you, is it, Miss Termagant? I wondered where you'd got to. I told that old fool Pope to leave room for you in case I needed my choppers."

Mr. Pope clicked some more and the dinner lady bawled in Mrs. Gorman's ear, "There's a place for Miss Adamson with the younger ones, dear. Don't worry—"

Mrs. Gorman's chin came forth belligerently.

"I'm not deaf even if you are! Didn't you hear me say I'd kept a place for her? Fetch her some soup, she's as skinny as a sparrow. And I'll have some more while you're about it." She passed up her plate with clawlike fingers, and the helper took it willy-nilly and bumbled off saying something about ingratitude. Mrs. Gorman showed me her gums.

"It's battered fish after. Crispy it is. Spoils it if you mangle it around too long. Just put them on my lap, lovie. That's it—I shan't need them for my soup but they'll be handy there."

I placed the teeth reverently on her floral rayon dress and leaned back to include Mr. Pope.

"Sorry to come between you two lovebirds," I said mostly to him. "But I could see you needed a chaperone and I wouldn't like you to give the place a bad name."

Granny loved it. She cackled and spluttered something about how he'd be lucky to get a chance. Poor old Pope rolled his right eye nervously in our direction but kept his head down to his soup. His neck became mottled and the amazing thought crossed my mind that maybe he did fancy Granny Gorman. And why so amazing? No more amazing than me fancying Doc Beamish. Granny didn't have teeth and I didn't have working legs. So what?

"I don't blame you." I leaned toward him confidentially. "She's something. Anyone can see that." He put down his soupspoon and rose to the fight. I stopped him, wide-eyed and placating. "Oh and I don't blame *her* either. I expect you've had trouble with women all your life, haven't you?"

"I'll thank you to mind your own business, young lady!" The loose skin under his chin wobbled like a turkey's. "Why don't you sit with your own age group and make your smart-aleck remarks to them?"

One half of me loved being spoken to like that. Like other fathers—or grandfathers—spoke to other sixteen-year-old girls. The other half trembled and cringed and wept. Granny Gorman came to my rescue.

"She's sitting here because I like her sitting here," she snapped, her chin nearly stabbing his eye. "And I like her smart-aleck remarks. They're better than

19

your silence any day. They make me feel I'm still alive. You make me feel I was buried last year!"

They tried to outstare each other in front of my face; then the helper arrived with two soup plates and my cutlery. They relapsed, both breathing audibly. It had doubtless done their respirations and hearts a lot of good, that little confrontation. And Granny at least had thoroughly enjoyed it.

We got on with our soup while Mr. Pope sat on huffily but not clicking. It was gorgeous soup. The fish arrived, nestling crisply in a bed of fluffy white creamed potatoes. There were peas and diced carrots in stainless steel dishes if you wanted them. Granny fitted her teeth behind her handkerchief while I smothered my plate in tomato ketchup. We ate without conversation, appreciatively. Mr. Pope scooped his fish from the batter shell, mashed it with a little of the potato and forked it slowly into his mouth. I waited until he put the fork down and drank some water.

"Don't you want your crispy outside?" I indicated the batter with a glance. "I'll eat it for you if you like."

He pushed his plate farther from me. "No thank you."

"Sorry. I just thought—"

Granny saw her chance and took up the cudgels again with alacrity.

"You just want to leave it to give Cook a guilty conscience—that's it, isn't it? You always have to leave something on your plate! Go on, let her have it—

she knows how to enjoy her food even if you don't. Go on—push it onto her plate. . . ." She reached across with her knife and scooped the flimsy batter over with deceptive speed.

"No, really . . ." I didn't want to be involved in an actual hand-to-hand battle on my second day. It might well be the first black mark that would lead to expulsion. "You have it, Mr. Pope. I didn't mean to deprive you."

A helper's face appeared, moonlike, hovering over us from behind.

"Any difficulties, Mr. Pope?" Upside down the honeyed smile was ghoulish. "We know about your appetite, but Cook does so hope that tonight she's tempted you to— Why Mr. Pope!" Genuine pleasure crept into the voice. "You've cleared your plate! Well done! Cook will be delighted. And the dessert is plain ice cream, so that should slip down a treat."

Mr. Pope hesitated, considering spilling the beans, then accepted temporary defeat.

"I don't want any ice cream," he said at last like a protest marcher hanging on to the last shred of his banner. "Nasty cold stuff to go to bed on."

Granny was indefatigable, teeth and chin so prominent they looked dislocated. "Helps blood pressure," she stated categorically. "You have some."

"I'll thank you, Mrs. Corman . . ." They started eyeing each other across me again and I tipped my head at the helper.

"Bring him a small helping," I said quietly. "I'll probably get him to eat it."

Granny and I split his ice cream between us and Granny produced from her tidy bag a battered bar of chocolate that we crumbled over the top. He ostentatiously didn't watch us, but he didn't entirely retreat into silence. When Granny asked him if he'd like a spoonful he sprang to the attack immediately.

"Not when it is covered in chocolate probably as old as you and even less hygienic!" he said with relish. He'd obviously spent a happy five minutes cooking up that remark and he couldn't resist smiling over it. Strangely enough, Granny liked it too and chortled as she popped the proffered spoonful into her own mouth. Then when we'd finished, along came the cook herself to tell Mr. Pope what a good, clever boy he was, and while she was doing that the helper congratulated me on persuading him to eat a proper meal.

"Older people can be shy about eating in front of youngsters," she told me, as much the amateur social worker as Aunt Nell. "But you certainly did wonders for these two. Look at Mrs. Gorman laughing."

I looked. Granny was almost apoplectic, and as I caught her eye I stopped feeling guilty and let the giggles start oscillating my diaphragm.

"And after all," went on the helper lugubriously, "what has she got to laugh about? What have any of us here got to laugh about . . . ?" She tried to turn the last bit into ruefulness but I was past taking offense. I snorted and snuffled to control incipient hysteria.

"You'd be surprised," I told her as she turned away. "You'd be really surprised!"

I only hoped that as well as black marks they put

silver or gold ones by your name at Thornton Hall. Because I must have earned myself two or three that night.

One of the night staff greeted me gaily in the corridor.

"You're the new girl—Frances, isn't it? Where would you like to go—games room, television, reading?"

"I'd like to go outside." I was in a good mood and I smiled at her. "And please call me Fran. I'm called Frances when I'm in trouble."

"Which isn't often, I hope." Gray eyes smiled at me sentimentally. "I'm Nurse Bennett. Just an auxiliary really. I answer to Bennie except when the head nurse is in earshot." She had a nice laugh. "You're not actually supposed to go outside after dinner, Fran. We've cleared up and locked the main doors and we like to start the baths as soon as possible."

"I have my bath in the morning. And I would love to see a bit of the garden." I put everything I had into a pleading look. "I came yesterday and I haven't had time to see outside. I really need some air."

She capitulated without a struggle. "Oh all right. This way. You can go out onto the terrace—there's a ramp from there to the main path. Have you got a watch?" We synchronized watches. "No more than half an hour, mind, otherwise you might find yourself locked out!" She looked soppy again. "The times I've said that to my daughter and she doesn't take a bit of notice."

She'd got a daughter about my age; she was going to be a soft touch.

"Because she knows you couldn't do it." I grinned at her cheekily, so that we both knew where we were, and followed her into the big room where I'd sat with Uncle Roger and Aunt Nell that afternoon. A series of big, old-fashioned French doors led onto the terrace and Nurse Bennett—Bennie—opened one with a clandestine air and stood aside while I shoved my way through.

"Half an hour," she whispered.

"Half an hour!" I agreed solemnly and trundled along the terrace without another glance at my watch.

There were masses of flowers. Honeysuckle waved its fronds over the stone balustrade, aubrietia pushed between the pot-bellied pillars, brown and yellow gaillardias marched alongside the ramp and beyond them were bushes of floribunda roses. I had scissors in my tidy bag, and I moved slowly cutting a flower here and there so that there were no gaps—I'd had experience of irate gardeners before. Soon my lap was piled with flowers. I came upon forget-me-nots growing wild behind a low box hedge and wedged a tight bunch between the frame and canvas of my chair. Then some giant cushions of lavender—and what better flowers than lavender for scenting a room? They were tougher and fitted on the other side of the chair.

The sun was gone by this time, and tangled skeins of gnats danced crazily over the dampening lawn. They reminded me of how I felt sometimes; they were a model of the constantly moving atom. I left the path and forced my wheels over the resilient turf to join them. The house looked lovely from here; the terrace floated above me, and the gray ribbon of the drive wound in a huge sweep from the other side of the house, girdling this lawn, the gnats, my flower-strewn chair on its way to the lodge and the main gates. Some of the windows were lit and I tried to find mine, but as there was no sign of the yellow swimming-pool roof I guessed it must be somewhere else. The sense of being on my own in all this gracious space was exhilarating and very unusual. I was happy and relaxed, but I hadn't lost the terrific sense of anticipation that had met me as I arrived yesterday in the ambulance. Slowly I leaned down and began to pick the shuttered daisies, and in the half-light I made a daisy chain and put it on my head.

How long I might have stayed there exulting I don't know, but just then a prosaic white ambulance revved up the incline from the gates and began the long parabola to the house. I watched it in the twilight and wondered whether it contained a new person to be investigated. Certainly its driver would see me and would report my strange presence.

With a sigh I started back to the terrace and the watching Bennie. She smuggled me and the flowers back to my room and brought me a selection of vases and jam jars and a seed catalogue with some gorgeous flower pictures for Zeek, the door. She said she'd look in at ten to make sure I'd got myself into my nightie and sanipads properly and she wouldn't be surprised if she didn't bring a nice cup of coffee and some custard cream biscuits with her.

Bennie was going to be the perfect ally. I began to sort my flowers on the table by my trunk. Dorothy watched me from her button eyes and looked very contented as the lavender, honeysuckle, rose and montbretia smell permeated the room.

"I've got to finish unpacking that trunk," I told her severely. "And there's all these flowers . . . and the door. . . . They won't let me keep my room private if I can't sort it out by tomorrow!"

Dorothy grinned at me. She didn't care about the chores. The night was long and neither of us was sleepy and the possibilities of Thornton Hall were endless.

3

AT MIDNIGHT, stimulated by Bennie's coffee, I was still sorting out my things, still waiting for something to happen. It was a shock—yet not a surprise—when the phone burped discreetly as internal phones do, waited to see if I was asleep before burping again. I got to it fast.

"Hello," I gasped. "Is that you, Bennie? I'm ready for bed and I'm just going so you don't have to—"

Granny Gorman's voice rasped across mine.

" 'Tisn't no good you trying to say anything, Miss Termagant. I can't hear on these things. But you're not asleep now, so can you come and get my choppers? You were in such a darned hurry to get out of the dining room I didn't have time to give them to you."

"I'm not supposed to. And my second night and all I don't want to make a bad impression."

"Can't hear you. I've cleaned 'em up nicely and they're here waiting. And I've found some more chocolate in my tidy bag."

The phone clicked horribly as she fumbled it back down. I could imagine her, chin like Punch's, sitting up in bed grinning at the carrot she'd offered me. Of course I was going. Nothing to do with the chocolate. I'd been waiting for an excuse like this.

The corridor was dimly lit and spooky with its dark oak and the emptiness like a presence. I thumbed my nose at it and paused to stare at Zeek. Already he was beautiful, with a line of flower pictures extending from handle level to floor. I'd have to get someone to do the top half for me. Bennie probably. He was going to be covered—absolutely covered. The first thing you'd see as you came out of the lift would be Zeek.

There were other doors on my corridor but none of them had numbers on so they must be cupboards or extra bathrooms or something. I wondered whether they'd given me an isolated room as a treat or to segregate me from the others. Whatever the reason, it *was* a treat.

I was on the ground floor before I realized that I didn't know Granny's room number. She'd be on this level—all the old people who were more or less mobile were on the ground floor—but there were probably a dozen or more rooms behind the communal ones, and probably patrolling night staff somewhere around. I paused, nibbling my lip and recalling the layout of other homes. There would be a list of names and corresponding room numbers somewhere near the kitchen possibly. That was in case anybody needed meals served in bed. It was my only hope. I bowled on toward the dining room; surely the kitchen wouldn't be too far from there. My wheels were soundless on the wide oak boards, my ears sang with the effort to hear anyone before they heard me. Just beyond the double doors, which I remembered concertinaed into the dining room, there was a narrow, dark passage turning to the left; a light over a door at the end. It was the kitchen, a new one doubtless made from the old morning room or something. On a bank of modern burners a kettle and pan of milk were steaming gently. The staff were going to have their midnight drink very soon.

I looked desperately around. There was a notice board with about a million lists on it. Menus, duty rosters, individual diet sheets—Mr. Pope had an ulcer so maybe he wasn't such a fusspot as I'd imagined—and at the top, almost out of my vision, a dozen neatly typed names aligned to neatly typed numbers. On the end in scribbly writing were two extra names. Frances Adamson, number seventy-eight, and right at the very bottom Lucas Hawkins, number five. Was he the new arrival in the ambulance that night? I zipped on up the list and found Granny next to Stella Graves. Number eleven. Number eleven. I kept muttering it in my mind though it was unforgettable anyway, then I backed off hastily, did a three-point turn by the array of sinks and shot back down the little passage and into the big shadowy hall where at least I could pretend I was looking for Bennie instead of sneaking food.

No one was about. In view of the kettle and milk saucepan it was surprising until I found room number five. Then a soothing voice from behind the door told me that Bennie had been waylaid on her way to make the hot drinks.

"Now . . . don't take on so, my love. . . . Why won't you let me get you a nice cup of coffee and take two more of your painkillers and—"

A savage voice interrupted her. "Because I can't live on bloody painkillers! Because I'm sick of being doped up to the eyeballs!"

I stopped and eavesdropped unashamedly. The voice was young and it hadn't occurred to me that someone called Lucas Hawkins could be under forty.

Bennie was almost weeping. "I understand my dear—of course I do"—as if she could. Or if she could, would it be for longer than she was actually in the room? Wouldn't she have to put such agonizing understanding from her when she went to make the coffee? "But why go without them *now*? At night when you're alone? Tomorrow when you're with the others—"

"I'm never with anyone else—it's just me and this . . ." I wondered where he was pointing? Legs? Arms? Or just the pain?

Bennie said, "You've come here so that you won't be *able* to shut yourself away like that. It's wrong. There are others here—"

30

"Other *cripples* d'you mean? Like me d'you mean? So that I won't feel odd man out d'you mean?" The laugh was unpleasant. "That really is funny. Like blind schools. Or places for the deaf and dumb. In the end no one sees, speaks or hears. Great. Just great."

"Don't be so bitter, my dear." Casey could have dealt with him. She'd have told him to shut up. Bennie didn't know what to say. "It's not like that. There are young people—and elderly—"

"Great again. I just stay on till I'm geriatric, is that it?"

Bennie changed tactics. "Look. I'm going to get you a nice hot drink and two painkillers. No don't argue, else I'll get Doctor Beamish and heaven knows he needs his rest." She went on but I didn't wait for the rest. Poor old Bennie, if she found me out of bed now she really would burst into tears.

I got along to number eleven all right and Granny Gorman wasn't a bit surprised to see me.

"Come on in, Miss Termagant," she called to my surreptitious knock. " 'Tisn't locked." I opened the door and shoved myself in. She was sitting in bed, the teeth huge and hideous on the bed table. "What's the good of locking when they've got a master key anyway?" Her nightie was like a shroud and her hair fell wispily around her face. No wonder Lucas Hawkins wasn't mad on being associated with geriatrics. She shifted irritably in bed. "What are you staring at girl? Say something."

I summoned a grin. "Can't get over how gorgeous you are with your hair undone and that seductive night attire."

31

She cackled. "Cheeky young devil. Wandering about the place all night. Could get into trouble."

I didn't answer. This would happen to me sometimes. I'd relax my self-protection for just a minute and the guts would ooze out of me somewhere—maybe the Achilles heel that I couldn't feel. I'd be like a jelly thinking, What's the use—what's the bloody *point*?

I guess it was listening to Lucas Hawkins and then seeing Granny sitting there like a gloating old witch; I don't know. Anyway I didn't say a word; I just pulled out a handful of tissues from her box and buried the teeth in them and stuck the whole lot in my tidy bag. I'd gone off the idea of being Keeper of the Teeth.

She knew. She was rummaging with silver paper around a lump of chocolate and she stopped and looked at me with her beady eyes.

"What's the matter, Miss Termagant—you're quiet."

I was going to say I couldn't speak till I'd been sustained with chocolate, but meeting that all-knowing gaze, I just said, "Don't you mind?"

"Mind?" The chin tucked itself in a bit and she looked slightly less evil. "Being old? Or having to depend on things like false teeth?"

I shrugged and wished I hadn't asked such a damned silly question.

She grinned again. "Course I mind. I'm still me inside this lot, you know." She stabbed at her chest with an arthritic finger. "Still May Gorman who could lead the blokes a fair dance." She stopped herself.

"Daft, isn't it? I feel just the same inside. Then I catch sight of myself in a mirror." She cackled. "Then for a bit my inside matches my outside."

"Yes." That was what had happened to me tonight. The bitter voice of Lucas Hawkins had been my mirror. And dammit, he was right—what was the point of keeping going with painkillers and things? What was the blasted *point*?

I focused Granny and said nastily, "Then I suppose you look at some of the others—the younger ones—and you think to yourself, Well at least I had my day. Is that how you cheer yourself up?"

She didn't seem to notice my bitchy tone. Her hairless brows drew together. "Doesn't work like that. They make me feel worse. The way they manage—their whole aim in life is just to manage. Social training or what ever the good doctor calls it. Have you seen that Penny Davis? No arms and she eats her meals better than old Pope!"

"I've seen her." And she'd made me feel guilty for being proud of my arms. I felt a bit better toward Granny and managed a watery grin.

A wheezy laugh blew the inverted lips out full size.

"No. Tell you what cheers me up. When a cheeky young miss comes along and whips my choppers for a joke. They don't make her feel sick—I don't make her feel sick. She talks to me as if she can still see May Gorman behind this lot"—another jab at her chest. "She lets me help her stir things up a bit. That's what cheers me up."

I stared at her. Maybe that was the point—to cheer

Granny Gorman up? I said slowly, "I've got wild plans for fixing up Staff Nurse Casey with Doctor Beamish."

She crowed delightedly. Then sobered. "You watch it, my girl. You could get into trouble. Real trouble. So they send you away."

I opened my eyes as wide as they would go. "Well, if you want me around to cheer you up, your job in life had better be to keep me out of trouble, wouldn't you say?"

"You're a cunning one, Miss Termagant." Granny shook her head, pleased again. "Think you're giving me an interest in life, eh? Well, you could be right." She shoved a piece of mangled chocolate at me. "Come on, have your treat and get back to bed. You'll be all eyes and no face tomorrow."

When I was a kid there was a zoo outing and a nine-year-old boy had pointed to the marmosets and yelled, "Look—they're like Frannie! Frannie looks like a monkey!" All eyes and no face.

I bit into my chocolate and said fearfully, "You don't think I look like a monkey, do you, Granny?"

Suddenly all the lines in her face sagged into quietness. She looked as old as the hills. And as good as the hills.

"I think you're beautiful." The lines leaped up and she was Mrs. Mephistopheles again. "But you act like a monkey. That's for sure. You certainly act like a monkey!"

I left her still cackling, and made cautiously for the lift. The ramp was a devil going back; I ought to have taken a run at it, but I was so darned tired all of a sudden. I was thankful Bennie had nagged me into washing and getting into my nightie earlier; the trunk would still have to wait. I just had strength to lift the arm of my chair and begin the business of edging myself over onto my turned-down bed next to Dorothy. It was good. The sheets smelled of the spray of lavender I'd tucked into them, and the other flowers smiled at me from all around the room. I settled back onto the high pillows with a sigh of contentment and reached for Dorothy. And then I remembered Lucas Hawkins.

I lay there thinking for a bit, not switching off the light.

Then I picked up the phone and pressed button number five.

A long burr sounded in my ear. Pause. Another burr. How many before I concluded he was asleep? How many had it taken me to cross the room from the table and . . . There was a click.

A voice said wearily, "You don't have to worry. I'm okay. Just leave me alone."

I said, "With pleasure. Tell me this first, Hawkins. Did you take the painkillers?"

"Who is that?"

"Did you take the painkillers?"

"I thought the one thing I'd get in this dead-end hole was privacy. Now I find there's some kind of Big Brother system working—"

"Cut the crap, Hawkins. Did you take the damn-and-blasted painkillers?"

"No." There was surprise in the monosyllable.

35

"Why not?"

"I don't have to tell you or anyone else that. Whoever you are." But he didn't put the phone down.

"Not anyone else. No. But me. Yes. Why didn't you take 'em?"

"Because I don't want to join the clan. Okay? I don't want to pretend I can be just as good as I was before. Now will you get off this phone and leave me strictly alone?"

"Sure. Like I said, with pleasure. One thing before I go, Hawkins. You did the right thing about the painkillers. Wrong motive, though."

"Hey?"

"You want to die, right? Well, let me tell you, boy. When you're hurting somewhere, you know for sure you're alive."

I put the phone gently down without saying good night and lay holding Dorothy and staring at the ceiling for a while before I put out my light.

4

  CASEY ROLLED MY wet draw-
sheet into the laundry basket, remade my bed, bathed
and dried me and wheeled me back to my room—
all in total silence.

"You're not much on the small talk, are you?" I
inquired pleasantly as I rummaged for one of my new
bras in the half-empty trunk.

"I've got plenty to say to you, my girl, when you're
dressed," Casey came back grimly, putting my jeans
and black T-shirt on the bed and kneeling to force
socks onto the legs which are attached to my torso
for some reason. "As for small talk. I didn't think
you needed it."

"I don't." I looked down at her carefully riotous
blond hair beneath the cap, the red nurse's hands

oddly at variance with her Marilyn Monroe figure and face. "Not the usual kind anyway. I'd like to know something about the new arrival in number five. And I'd also like to know whether Doctor Beamish is married. Plus—who is Uncle Roger and Aunt Nell's other adopted niece or nephew?"

She took it all without batting an eyelid. Stood up, whipped the bra out of its cellophane and snapped, "Get on with it. You'll be late for breakfast and I've got other people to—"

"You don't have to tell me. I'll find out anyway."

She said woodenly, "Doctor Beamish is unmarried. I don't know anything about number five. He came in after I'd gone off duty last night. And Mr. and Mrs. Parrish regularly visit Timmy Royston, who is now in the sanatorium."

"Thanks. Concisely put. I think I'll visit the sanatorium this morning and get Timmy's opinion on Aunt Nell's hot flushes."

"I don't think you will."

She said it flatly as she passed me my jeans and stood aside, watching me crouch and fumble into them. I knew what that meant. Uncle Roger and Aunt Nell would be adopting a new nephew any day now. I hesitated only a moment. Death is merciful in places like Thornton Hall, and I accepted it most of the time, but it *was* depressing to find that two places were vacated so quickly. I tugged my jeans fiercely upward and began to rock from side to side to get them up to my waist.

"The new arrival is rather—er—like, premature,

isn't he?" I asked. After all, if Timmy Royston was still conscious it couldn't cheer him up much to know his room was already filled.

She laid out my brush and comb and tidied the dressing table with a few swift, efficient movements that were a pleasure to see.

"Not very," she said in the same expressionless voice. Then she went to the door and picked up the laundry basket. "Now it's my turn. You've been here three days, Frances, and already I know of three . . . mistakes . . . you've made."

"Mistakes?" I opened my eyes very wide, knowing darn well I looked like an orphaned marmoset.

She ignored that. "You have acquired a set of false teeth which aren't yours. You have eaten too many sweet things when you know you are on a strictly regulated diet. And you have been outside after hours."

My marmoset expression disappeared in sheer horrified incredulity at the treachery of the two people I'd counted as friends.

"Tittle-tattle," I spluttered. "You've been listening to tittle-tattle without giving me a chance to defend myself!"

She smiled grimly. How did anyone like Marilyn Monroe manage to smile grimly?

"Not so fast, Frances. You threw a bundle of tissues into the waste bin just now. I heard them clunk and fished them out. Did you forget you'd wrapped a set of dentures in them?" She held them up triumphantly. One to Casey. "And certainly I listen when Nurse

Bennett tells me Mr. Pope cannot sleep because he is hungry. And when she refused him a hot drink, he had to tell her about missing half his dinner. You see, Frances, he has an ulcer and—"

"*I* know," I said impatiently, scoring her another point for that. "And then poor old Bennie's conscience grew heavier and heavier, so she had to mention to you also that she'd let me out into the garden when she shouldn't have done."

Casey raised swallowtail brows. "Not at all. You're jumping to conclusions again, Frances. Look around you and use your brains. When I left you yesterday afternoon, this room was empty of flowers. Now it is full. Also you have not finished unpacking."

I took a deep breath. Three out of three to Casey.

"Listen. I can explain everything. I'm not some kind of klepto nut. Give me the teeth and I'll return them. It was a joke—just a joke. And the extra dessert last night . . . another joke." I wondered what would happen if she knew about Granny's crumbly chocolate. "Honestly. It was just that Mr. Pope was being bloody minded about his food. He wouldn't have had the ice cream anyway, so I thought . . . Oh Casey, it wasn't im*portant.*"

"It would be if it became a regular habit." She didn't give me the teeth. They looked obscene nestling in the palm of her hand. "And what about stripping the garden of flowers?"

"Stripping the—" I closed my mouth and swallowed. "Listen. If you can find one place—one solitary place—bare of flowers in that garden, I'll give you

40

first prize. Okay, so I sinned. I went out after the doors had been locked. But there are enough flowers in that garden to fill every room in Thornton Hall and then some over. And please forget what I said about Bennie," I concluded swiftly.

She leaned over to my dressing table, took some tissues, rewrapped Granny's dentures and dropped them in her pocket. Then she said, "You make it sound very lighthearted Frances. Maybe it is. But in a place like this we make rules for very good reasons. And our main one is self-discipline." She swept me with her cool blue eyes and I was conscious that I hadn't buttoned my flies yet, my shirt was in a bunch over the new bra and my hair uncombed. "I suggest after breakfast you come back here and see to your room. That is if you still wish it to be private. If you can't cope, I'll get you some help."

"I can cope," I said fiercely. "They promised me I could say myself when the cleaners could come in."

"You have to *show* us you can cope," she said, as if I hadn't spoken. "And you won't have long because you're due in the physio room at ten sharp. And after that it's O.T. till lunch."

Occupational therapy. Dreary, dreary, dreary.

"What's the good of having a swimming pool and a garden and a games room if they make you do O.T. all the time?" I whined.

"Shut up and get cracking," she returned. And left.

I followed her to the door, tugged Zeek open and yelled down the corridor, "Why don't you go and tell Doc Beamish about my 'mistakes'?" She didn't

41

even look back. "It would be a chance for you two to get together!" I was provoked and childish. "He might not stay unmarried for long! He might not stay *here* for long! Gather ye rosebuds while ye may. Grab your opportunities as they arise—" The lift doors swished shut and she was gone. I put my head on Zeek's smooth chest and knew I'd been cheap. My self-respect was in the dust.

Granny wasn't at breakfast, so I couldn't tell her about losing her teeth. I ate with Stella Graves and Penny Davis. They didn't know anything about Lucas Hawkins. They couldn't talk about anything except the O level tests, which they were in the midst of preparing for. They were to have history all that afternoon, and they recited the 1832 Reform Act like a catechism while they managed their cornflakes and scrambled eggs with an adroitness that was horribly fascinating. I got back to my room as quickly as I could and began to put my stuff away in earnest. Dorothy watched me smugly, saying, "I told you what would happen." Even Zeek groaned approval when I left to go to physio and sealed him carefully against all intruders.

Miss Hamlin, the physio lady, was nice. They always are. She gave me rolling exercises—I hadn't done those before—and then five minutes in the sculling machine; as I pulled the oars, my legs pumped back and forth. Didn't do anything for them, but was supposed to keep the circulation going around the rest of me. It was fun. There was a kid there, a boy who looked about seven, having massage. He kept grinning at me. I asked him how many people there were at Thornton Hall and he said fifteen. That meant I'd still got at least six to meet not counting Lucas Hawkins and Timmy Royston.

He said, "We're in sort of threes. There's me and Timmy and Rosie. Then there's you and Stella and Penny. Then there's Henry and Mr. McGhie and Mrs. Tirrell. Then there's Mr. Pope and Mrs. Gorman and Mrs. Jarrett. I'm Dennis Makepeace."

"Dennis the menace," I panted, tugging at the oars and watching my knees rise up and down, up and down. "That makes twelve. Who are the last three?"

He looked nonplussed. "No one else. Twelve then. I'm not good at math."

"No." That made Lucas Hawkins the thirteenth. For a while. "I'm not much better myself. I wonder if I can guess how old you are. Ummm. Thirty-two and a half. Maybe thirty-three in August."

Dennis shook like a jelly beneath Miss Hamlin's capable hands.

"Eight and three quarters," he crowed. "How old are you?"

I stopped rowing, picked up my towel delicately and mopped myself.

"Two years older than Juliet when she met Romeo," I told him gravely.

"You're nuts." He giggled. "Are you going to school now?"

Miss Hamlin came over and lifted me into my chair.

"Frances is going to have a chat with Doctor Beamish now, Dennis," she said, smiling. "You'll see her

43

later." She turned to me. "Do you know your way, dear?"

I nodded vigorously. I didn't but I could find out. I glanced fairly coldly at Dennis Makepeace.

"Didn't you hear me say I was sixteen?" I asked. "I gave up school at Christmas. Or perhaps it gave me up."

Miss Hamlin said firmly for his benefit, "Frances will be in O.T. while you're having your lessons, young man. We don't waste our time at Thornton Hall, school or no school!" If she thought that was one in the eye for me she was wrong. That is one thing I have never done. Wasted my time.

Doc Beamish was painfully thin; his eyes were coal-black buttons sunk deep into a face that seemed all long jawbone and thin curly mouth. His desk looked like a stall at a jumble sale and his wiry hair stood on end where he combed it with his fingers. He certainly needed Casey.

He smiled warmly and shook my hand.

"Hullo again, Frances. I'm sorry I didn't get around to seeing you yesterday. How are you settling in?"

"Fine. Actually I don't have to see a doctor every day. You checked me on arrival."

"Oh I know you're as strong as a horse and very independent." His smile changed to a grin. "I don't want to see you as a doctor. Just as another member of the family."

It was the funniest thing. If Aunt Nell had said that I'd have cringed inside. Him I just wanted to punch

44

gently on the nose. With affection. And why was that? I popped the question into cold storage for future examination. Then swallowed, wondering whether I dared be cheeky to the boss man.

"Well, hi there, Brother Beamish," I ventured. "How were you yesterday?"

His black eyes stopped looking at a paraplegic and saw me.

"Snowed under with paperwork, which I hate." He drew his chair from behind the desk and straddled it in front of me. "More details from you, please, Frances. How are you managing in that room on the top? Would you prefer something more accessible?"

"I love it up there. The whole floor to myself."

"Actually the staff are always up there in the night for clean linen and things. Not so private as you might think."

"You know what I mean. I've called my door Zeek and I'm covering him with flowers. Is that okay?" Nothing like going straight to the top for permissions and things.

He was pleased. He grinned again. "Go to it, Frances. That room is yours. Period."

Honestly, I could have fancied him myself. I said, "Don't call me Frances. That's for when I'm on the mat. Fran. Call me Fran."

"Okay, Fran. Now what about the others? I know you didn't want formal introductions all around, but I hope you're getting to know the people outside your immediate age group."

"I know Granny Gorman quite well. Mr. Pope a

bit. Dennis Makepeace. I know Nurse Bennett pretty well too. And Casey of course."

"Casey?"

"Staff Nurse Casey. The gorgeous one. She looks like Marilyn Monroe."

"We've got a nurse who looks like Marilyn Monroe? You must be joking, Fran."

"I'm not. Your trouble is you don't see anyone unless they're in wheelchairs or on the physio couch. You should look at Casey. She's really something." What a sacrificing masochist I was!

He refused to be impressed. "Penny and Stella are pretty stunning too, don't you think?" He meant it. He really meant it.

I nodded soberly. I knew they were attractive girls but my mind couldn't get past those frightful hands fastened almost straight onto their shoulders. "Clever with it too. They're in the middle of O levels. It was the 1832 Reform Act before breakfast."

He laughed through his nose. Not much of a laugh, but he was probably out of practice.

"Terrific," he said.

"Oh I dunno." I was very casual. "You did O levels I suppose? Then A's. Then medical school."

His smile died. He stared at me levelly.

"If you think I'm maudlin about Penny and Stella, think again, Fran."

"I don't think that." I stared straight back at him. "You're saying the wrong words but I don't think that."

"There's a difference between compassion and pity."

I was immensely relieved. "That's it. Sure. I couldn't think what it was. You're not outside looking in. You're right here." I grinned at him and thank God he grinned back slightly. "But listen, Brother Beamish, if you feel compassion for Stella and Penny, feel it for yourself. Okay? You're not in a wheelchair and you've got a pair of arms. But I guess you're handicapped in other ways."

He stared at me for a long time with those round black eyes of his. Then he let his breath go in a gasp of surrender.

"You're a screwball, Fran. They told us that from the last place. Said you couldn't be organized. Things like that. I thought we might be glad of you."

I said vigorously, "Glad of me? Christ, you *need* me!"

This time his laugh was much more than a snort and I wheeled myself to the door before it went to my head.

"Hey, have we finished talking?" he asked, hands on the back of his chair, chin on hands. "I was going to suggest you have a go at some O levels next year. Or a shorthand-typing course."

Was he trying to tell me something? That I'd got a year? Even two?

I opened the door and frowned heavily. "You haven't been listening to me. I'm far too busy just now for anything like that."

He laughed again. "I'll let you off for a while then. But you'll have to do O.T., Fran."

Thank God he let it go. I didn't want to have to come into the open and inform him that even if I

47

had as long as three years, he must be bonkers if he thought I'd waste that time at a school desk!

I pulled a ghastly face. "Why? If I'm skidding around the place looking happy I'm a great advertisement."

"You can still skid, in between O.T. sessions."

"And physio. And baths. And meals." I moved my head from side to side in a gorgeous Jewish way I'd cultivated after I saw *Fiddler on the Roof.* "I should be so lucky."

He kept laughing. Before I could really start getting any ideas about him, I said, "Do one thing for me, Brother Beamish, will you?"

"What's that?"

"Take a look at Casey next time your paths cross."

He shook his head despairingly. "All right, all right."

"A good look," I persisted.

"Get out!" he ordered.

I bet he hadn't said that to anyone in a wheelchair before. It made me feel best of all. I trundled down the corridor toward the O.T. room with an idiotic smile all over my face. I'd got back my self-respect, all right.

That night I dialed five at just past midnight. It rang once.

He said, "Who the hell are you? Do you make a habit of ringing people up in the night when they're getting some sleep?"

"No. I didn't want to disappoint you. Had some painkillers today?"

"Yes!"

"Good. I knew you'd see sense."

His blood pressure built up along the wire. "I thought you congratulated me last night for not taking the blasted things?"

I said piously, "You don't take 'em and you know you're still here. Then you take 'em to make here bearable."

"You've got an answer for everything, Miss Clever Clogs. So . . . what's your name?"

"Nothing," I came back as obscurely as possible. "Don't put the phone down. I've got something to say. I need help."

"Is that possible?"

"Sure. Not even God can manage without help. Listen. There's a nurse here. Interested in Doc Beamish. She'd be great for him. What do I do?"

There was a long pause. He said quietly, "You're a nurse. Matchmaking. Christ."

Before I could put him wise he replaced the receiver at his end with a gentleness that had finality about it.

5

O.T. WASN'T BAD. Of course Granny Gorman and Mrs. Jarrett knitted like crazy and poor old Pope fiddled with a marquetry picture. But Mrs. Tirrell, who turned out to be about thirty with a face like a horse but a nature to go with it, was doing some gorgeous petit-point stuff on a frame. And the other two blokes were knocking up matching stools. And they were all nice and chatty in a reserved sort of way about the last budget and whether Bristol was going to be able to pay for its new dock. That is except Granny and me; we sat and hatched plans for the recovery of her teeth and the imminent nuptials of Casey and Beamish, like a pair of witches, until Mrs. Pountney—the head O.T. herself—suggested that as I did not seem to be able to knit perhaps

I'd like to take a tour of the rooms and see what else they had to offer. She came with me and it was a nice surprise to find there was a potter's wheel, painting equipment of all kinds, a spinning wheel and loom—things like that. Best of all, the sports room and swimming pool were under her wing, and as the weather was so marvelous I decided straightaway that swimming was what I wanted to do during my O.T. sessions. She smiled and agreed, probably thinking I'd soon get fed up with the chore of changing and drying and so on.

Most of the kids swam or spent a lot of time splashing. Dennis Makepeace, Penny, Stella, a tiny girl almost completely paralyzed called Rosie Jimpson, besides two or three kids from local schools who were doing projects about those "less fortunate than themselves." Ha. Ha. Ha. But all of them had schoolwork as well, so a lot of the time I had the pool to myself. It was marvelous. Swimming is my favorite thing. Water is the great equalizer. When Doc Beamish dived in one day, we moved together unhampered by wheelchairs and I knew my legs trailing behind me were no longer heavy and ugly. My beautiful arms and hands were so strong; I reached forward and pulled the water toward me; went under; came up; turned my head to smile at him delightedly.

He watched me pull myself onto the rubber raft. He trod water, his face still and watching.

"What's up?" I spluttered, hoping to God I wasn't obviously wetting myself.

He steadied the raft.

51

"It occurred to me then. The way you swam then pulled yourself up there and rolled over. That's how mermaids must get onto flat rocks when they want to sun themselves."

Now I ask you. Has any girl, whole or not, had a better compliment than that? I looked down at my legs. I didn't hate them, because they were like a mermaid's tail; that was the first time I'd looked at my legs and not hated them.

But what to say to Beamish? It had to be something to show my appreciation; my grand acceptance of the compliment as due to a woman of my . . . er . . . charm. I was, after all, two years older than Juliet when she met Romeo. So I giggled.

However, by the time Casey peeled off my swimsuit and chucked a rough towel at me I was feeling so smug it was sickening.

"You'd better watch out," I told her severely when she bent to rub at my feet. "The way things are going I'm getting ahead of you."

She said, "Rub your hair for Pete's sake. And Mr. Ottwell says he's put fresh flowers for you in the greenhouse."

"Listen, I like to pick my own flowers," I protested. Mr. Ottwell was the gardener and had been grudgingly cooperative about my daily flower picking.

She shrugged. She didn't believe in idle chatter.

I toweled and reached for my bra. "I said I was getting ahead of you. Don't you want to know how?"

She looked at me with a sort of humorous resignation that was intimate for Casey. "How?" she queried obediently.

"Brother Beamish. He's looking at me. Seeing me."
She stopped putting on my socks and her look stopped being resigned. She waited a long while and in spite of my bravado I felt quaky. You can only take the enfant-terrible bit so far.

At last she said slowly, "Am I supposed to be jealous, Frances?"

It sounds snide as I write, but it wasn't. It was a genuine question.

I was breathless. "Is it possible for someone like you to be jealous of someone like me?"

She nodded. She didn't get up or go on with my socks. I had her complete attention.

"Oh yes." She spoke dead seriously. "Quite possible."

She was looking at me exactly as one attractive woman might look at another.

I gasped a laugh. "Don't be daft, Casey. You know Brother Beamish better than me. Besides, even if . . ." Suddenly I was angry with her. Angry for making me feel like an attractive woman. "Even if he did fancy me—there's no future . . . is there?"

Now her eyes would flicker and look away. But she didn't budge. She was as steady as a rock.

"You know better than that, Frances. It's by no means unusual for paraplegics to marry. A doctor would be an excellent choice for obvious reasons."

I stared back into her beautiful, level, blue eyes. She didn't pussyfoot around, Casey. She was brutally honest. Which meant that she didn't know everything. The all-knowing, honest-if-brutal Casey did not know everything. I loved Beamish all over again for not spreading around my entire case history. It meant that Casey and I were even again—because after all what sort of handicap are lousy legs if they look like a mermaid's tail? Yes, everything was sunny again. I was in control, with the excitement bubbling up. I was the puppet master manipulating away with confidence.

"Then . . ." I paused ponderously. "Then, yes, you *should* be jealous, Casey dear," I said softly. "I think he's terrific. And today he told me I was like a mermaid. Remember the Lorelei? Sitting there on her rock, luring the blokes?"

She grinned unexpectedly. Her teeth were lovely.

"You should have lived in the time of the Medici, Fran. You love intrigue, don't you?"

"Changing the subject? Don't you believe me? You should."

"Okay, so he said something nice. Why not? You're an attractive girl. It's the way you're using the incident to get me going." There. She'd as good as admitted that she had a yen for Beamish. "You're as calculating as—"

"As you, Casey?" I asked with marmoset innocence.

She'd had enough. "Do your own socks!" She stood up and practically flounced out of the changing room, and I wondered whether I'd rushed things a bit much and lost her to her protective ice world. But when I trundled into the greenhouse to see Mr. Ottwell, he said, "I took them flowers in for the house. That Staff Nurse Casey just bin to see me and says you'd rather pick your own. All I ask is—leave the dahlias alone and go sparing on the asters."

"Yippeee!" I turned my chair around on the spot and Mr. Ottwell grabbed a teetering flowerpot and looked frightened to death. "Thank you—thank you—thank you! I'll stick to moon daisies and lavender, okay?" I spun myself again. "D'you know what? She isn't cold and calculating at all. She'll be great for Brother Beamish!"

Ottwell looked sour. "I don't know what you're on about, but if you're going to twirl that ruddy chair again, go outside to do it. It'll make my tomatoes giddy, that will."

He pushed me outside and went back grumbling. But he knew as well as I did that tomatoes thrive on twirling wheelchairs.

It was Sunday again and Aunt Nell and Uncle Roger took turns to play me at table tennis. They'd wanted to take me out in the car and I'd said no. I don't know why. The summer sky had turned a copper color that morning, and the air felt prickly on my skin. I wore a halter top and a long seersucker skirt, and because of the thinness of it I thought I could smell myself. Casey, who would have told me not to be so stupid, had a day off and her relief was a tall, angular woman who believed in my fretful complaints and larded the deodorant talc on so that by lunchtime it was a thick paste beneath my rubber pants.

Aunt Nell was disappointed at me turning down her suggestion.

"We were looking forward to showing you the house," she said. "There's a nice view of the sea from the sitting room."

"I don't call the Bristol Channel the sea," I said rudely.

Aunt Nell subsided but Uncle Roger said equably, "Water then. It has boats on it, you know. The occasional skier. Children at its edge. And it would be cool on a day like this."

I said contrarily, "I'm not a bit hot. Let's play table tennis. It's so boring just sitting talking."

So we played and I beat them both. That was possible with Aunt Nell, who was top-heavy, but not with Uncle Roger. I was really annoyed with him for letting me win.

Aunt Nell panted exaggeratedly and said, "Can we go and sit outside, Frances dear? It's rather close indoors, don't you think?"

"Okay." I bowled ahead of them and said over my shoulder in parentheses, "I was hoping to take you upstairs to see my room, but if you'd rather go outside that's okay."

Aunt Nell dithered about on the terrace. "Frances dear. How perfectly sweet of you. What shall we do, Roger? We could talk just as easily upstairs."

Was Uncle Roger getting at me when he said firmly, "There's plenty of time for Fran to see our house and for us to see her room. Let's make the most of the grounds while we can." I felt him take the handle of my chair, and try as I would I couldn't outstrip him. I relapsed sulkily and let them walk me down to the big horseshoe-shaped lawn where I'd sat my first night covered in flowers. They pushed me into the shade of an aspen and sat on the grass in front of me. Uncle Roger folded himself fairly neatly in the middle. Aunt Nell got down in lumbering stages like a camel. They looked portentous.

I decided immediately on the disarming approach.

"Look. I'm sorry. I know I'm being beastly and I'm sorry. It's something to do with the drugs. Every so often they have to cut them down before I blow my mind, and then I get irritable and—" I recalled with exquisite clearness how exciting every new day had been last week, and the thought that it was probably just drugs made me want to cry. I finished desolately, "I suppose this is the real me. I'm dreary and cross. I should be doing something constructive like Penny and Stella instead of bumming around kidding myself I can make life happen." Aunt Nell was rearing up on her knees preparatory to taking me in her arms. I waved her down. "Please don't. I'll only be rude again and upset you." A large tear rolled down my nose and plopped off the end, doubtless giving the impression of snot "You're such good people. But you see I've always been surrounded by good people. So I can't help inclining toward the others a little bit. Granny Gorman and Casey . . . not that they're evil or anything, but they've got a pretty good veneer. You can bang on it and it doesn't crack. Not often anyway. But you—when I'm horrid to you, I know it hurts you and sometimes that gives me a kick. . . . Oh God, I must be a bloody sadist or something!" And I howled into the neck of my halter.

They were marvelous. They didn't say a word— perhaps they were scared to—but they made noises and Uncle Roger's big hanky was wielded to good purpose and when I surfaced five minutes or so later, they each had a hand on my feet. They knew I couldn't feel that. It was a gesture of friendship and nothing more.

"I'm sorry," I muttered.

Uncle Roger took over. "We are too. Maybe if we'd had kids we'd be a bit more tactful at times. I don't know." He sat up straight and blew out a deep breath. "Let's forget it, Fran—at least put it behind us for now. We understand each other better, so it's a good thing it happened. But we do want to talk to you. We thought if you came home with us—put Thornton Hall at a distance—we might be able to plan something. But we can at least talk about it now." He was being portentous again. It wasn't really like him and I got frightened.

"It's about the rules, isn't it? Self-discipline and all that?"

Aunt Nell actually smiled. So did Uncle Roger.

"Nothing like that, Fran. Quite the opposite." He settled himself in a new position, legs crooked, arms clasping knees. They both looked most uncomfortable. "First of all, you'll be sorry to hear that little Timmy Royston died yesterday."

The way he said it. Passing regret. Would he talk like that when—if—I . . . ? Then I looked at Aunt Nell and saw her blue eyes full of pain and her mouth thin and haggard.

Uncle Roger read my thoughts. "Your Aunt Nell was with him," he said matter-of-factly.

58

Unexpectedly, I liked the way he gave me Aunt Nell. Your Aunt Nell. The ever-anxious eyes, the cumbersome figure, they were valuable because they were mine. After all, she was just as a mother should be. She was made for motherhood and to all intents and purposes I had no mother. I forced myself to reach down and touch her shoulder, and thank goodness she didn't even look at me, just bowed her head and stared down at the daisies she and Uncle Roger were busily crushing.

He continued levelly, "Things have to go on, Fran. Our new 'nephew' is called Lucas Hawkins. He's eighteen. Accident on his motorbike. Lost both legs." He tried to make it sound clinical. "His parents are banking on Thornton Hall."

Lucas Hawkins was my secret. I wasn't keen on him being put under the microscope like this. And I was less keen on what was revealed there.

I said, "I don't get it. He can learn to walk on tin legs, can't he? I thought this was a residential place. And if he's got parents why are you adopting him?"

Aunt Nell burst out, "That's what's so awful, Frances dear. He won't see them—won't see any of his relatives. It's all wrong—he's retreated right into himself."

"He's probably in a lot of pain," I reminded her shortly.

Uncle Roger took over again. "Aunt Nell means that no one can get to him to help him. We know he can't help pushing everyone away, Fran, but the fact remains. It's a problem."

59

I didn't say anything. My mind was going around this unexpected information and I could feel interest stirring inside me again. Because of my mood, it manifested itself as resentment. He had been okay then, this Lucas Hawkins. Walking about, playing football, riding a motorbike. He hadn't been born like it. He was different from most of us. I could see it made it worse for him, but I couldn't forget the cool contempt in his voice the last time he'd spoken on the phone. The way he'd made me feel small and petty.

I said stubbornly, "I still don't see why he's here. We're mostly congenital and anyway we're here for always. It *is* our home."

Uncle Roger put his chin on his knees. "His people are very rich, Fran. They heard about Thornton Hall and the work Doctor Beamish does. As I said before, it's their last hope."

Another silence while I digested this. Rich. It put a new slant on things. Rich and spoiled. Speeding on a motorbike bought for him outright. Yuk.

I said, "But they can't buy him new legs, huh?"

Aunt Nell pleaded. "Frances dear. That isn't what they wanted when they thought of Thornton Hall. They wanted peace of mind for him. Acceptance of his disability."

"So they send him to a home for the physically handicapped. Where every day it's rammed home to him what he's got to live with."

Uncle Roger tried to speak but Aunt Nell couldn't stop now.

"Frances. Dear. You don't realize because you live

60

here. That's why we wanted to take you away for a while. Like standing on top of a hill and seeing things in perspective sometimes. It's the *spirit* here. It's wonderful. It makes you feel humble." Her eyes filled with tears and I shifted mine away fast. Our moment of communion was past.

Uncle Roger tried to bring the emotional temperature down.

"The only thing is, it hasn't worked. He's been here a week and he won't move from his room." He spoke drily, as if we were discussing the foibles of English weather.

"Stalemate," I suggested.

"Exactly." His gray eyes weren't so wishy-washy after all. They were very clear. "That's where you come in, Fran."

"Me?" Wasn't it just what I'd wanted? Hadn't I already tried to muscle in anyway? "Not likely. Not Pygmalion likely in fact."

"Frances. *Dear*—"

"You're the same age group," Uncle Roger went on as if neither of us had spoken. "In many ways you're older than him. And he could never suspect you of pitying him—condescending to him. You could get him interested again."

Yet another silence while I digested this too.

I said slowly, "How could I interest him, Uncle Roger?"

He said lightly, "Come on, Fran, that's obvious. You can interest him as any beautiful young woman might interest a young man."

The excitement was back. Without drugs and under that heavy copper sky, it was there again. I decided to ignore the beautiful part. I didn't want Aunt Nell reassuring me and Uncle Roger seeing with his clear gray eyes how horribly, terrifyingly self-conscious I was. I don't mean shy. I mean conscious of self. Because that's sinful somehow, isn't it? So I accepted the buried compliment though I knew that any beauty I possessed was the odd, orphaned-marmoset type.

I decided to be outraged.

"Do you mean I've got to *seduce* him? Don't you think that's tasteless to say the least? A paraplegic going all out for—"

Aunt Nell interrupted with a moan of physical pain. "Frances. Dear. You know we don't mean any such thing."

Uncle Roger spoke judiciously with humor in his voice.

"Face up to it, dear." He knew I was making fun of them, and he was playing my game. "In a way that's what we are asking. The strongest human urge next to hunger is sex. And we're asking Fran to use this—"

Aunt Nell's expression was beseeching. "Stop, Roger! I can't bear it. This is wrong. We shouldn't have listened to Doctor Beamish—we simply cannot ask Fran—"

"Doctor Beamish?" I was onto it; a cat on a mouse. "Do you mean to tell me Brother Beamish suggested this piece of skulduggery?"

The plot was definitely thickening. I didn't know

whether to be pleased or not at this fresh evidence
that Beamish had observed me during our swim.

Uncle Roger knelt up suddenly. "Not quite like that,
Fran. But he did think you might be able to bring
Lucas out of his hole. However, until he decides to
emerge from his room the idea is hypothetical. Let's
forget it. I suggest we get permission for you to stay
out late. Come on. Come to our place. I want to show
you the sea."

He was crafty, was Uncle Roger. He'd cut the conversation short at a point where he knew I'd do nothing but think about it. But I played him at his own
game anyway.

"Okay. On second thought I'd like that. It's getting
close here."

Uncle Roger grinned, remembering I'd denied the
heat only half an hour ago. But Aunt Nell was ingenu-
ously thrilled. She galloped over the lawn to see
Beamish and collect my cardigan. She was a bit like
our two daft dogs. Honest and straightforward and
imagining everyone else was the same.

I said abruptly over my shoulder to Uncle Roger,
"She must be tired. Up all last night like that."

He said, "She never gets tired. Not my Nell."

Now she was his. I watched her broad rear as it
went up the ramp to the terrace. She was made for
motherhood; she could have belonged to four or five
kids all at once.

It rained when we got to Clevedon, and I watched
the storm from their window on the Victorian front
as it whipped the sea into waves and then a heaving

63

spewing mass. Everything was gray. The sea, the houses, the sky, the broken pier. The string of fairy lights above the railings was tossed back and forth like a skipping rope, and as it grew darker there was a dull red glow on the horizon that was the blast furnaces over in Wales.

It excited me to near fever pitch. It made me yearn, too. I wanted to be one with the storm. I wanted to go out and get wet so that my eyes glazed like a seal's eyes and my hair was like a seal's skin. And I wanted something else too but I didn't know what. Something was waiting for me, just around the corner. Would I never find it?

Aunt Nell conjured a small intimate dinner onto the round table in the window. Clear soup, a gorgeous crab salad with lemon dressing, ice-cream meringue. I entertained them with Granny's plots for getting back her teeth. They laughed and we were close-knit and happy.

And all the time, outside in the darkness and the storm, something was waiting.

6

 WELL OF *course* I thought
about Lucas Hawkins.

At one minute past midnight I rang number five.
The rain had settled down to a steady drumbeat on
my dormer window; I felt safe yet besieged.

He didn't answer for ages. He knew it was me and
he thought I was some crummy scheming nurse. I
began to get nervous. If he wasn't going to answer,
how long dared I let it ring? I mean, once I replaced
my receiver I was admitting he'd won . . . and I
couldn't ring again could I? Maybe I could just leave
it off all night? But then all he'd have to do would
be lift it at his end and it would be stalemate.

I was filled with relief when it clicked and his voice
said, "You again. I thought I'd put a stop to you."

"You did. But I had to tell someone. I might have found the answer. It's so incredibly corny you'll want to throw up."

"What are you talking about?"

"Casey and Beamish of course. They're my project. I told you."

I heard him sigh. Then, incredibly, he said, "I've been thinking about it."

"You have?" He'd actually put his mind to matchmaking schemes? He'd actually got outside his own body, outside his room?

He said, "You're tricky. Very tricky. You couldn't care less about this nurse-doctor business. Perhaps you *are* this Casey character. And you think I might just be curious enough to come out and size you up."

I was so mad I nearly choked. Somehow I turned it into a laugh.

"How wrong can you be? Gosh if I was Casey . . ." Wistfulness cracked my voice. "Anyway, I'm not Casey. And I'm not Beamish either before you try any more funnies. And I'm interested in the two of them because it's better than being interested in . . . anything else."

"Horseshit," he said and waited expectantly.

I had to laugh again. "Yeah. Maybe you're right there. I *am* more interested in me than anyone or anything else."

"Don't apologize," he said drily.

"I'm not apologizing. I *am* interesting. And to prove it I'll tell you how I made a breakthrough with Casey."

I took a breath. "I made her jealous. How's that?"

"Like you said, so corny I could throw up."

"So what does it matter if it works? And does it or does it not prove that I am interesting?"

"You needn't be interesting. You could simply have a nice pair of legs."

"*Christ!!*"

It was as if a knife came up from under my ribs. The pain was awful and I put down the phone and leaned over it fighting a very real nausea. The rain drummed. I breathed deeply, counting each breath in and out, pushing a little extra out each time to make room in my lungs for a bigger intake. Beneath my nightie the things called legs hung flaccidly, newly washed and powdered, a useless responsibility I had to drag about with me. I closed my eyes tight shut and tried to remember that they were a mermaid's tail.

The rain drummed. I reached for Dorothy and behind me Zeek guarded my back. I was safe. Safe.

And then the phone burped discreetly.

I stared at it. He didn't know who I was. He didn't have my number. It must be dear Bennie wondering whether I was awake and would like tea or coffee. I picked it up gingerly. No one spoke.

"Hello." I tried to sound utterly sleepy, as if I'd just been wakened from three solid hours of total unconsciousness. But he knew.

"I've tried every damned number. Woken everyone in the blasted hospital. But not you—you weren't asleep. So don't pretend."

I said furiously, "It's not a hospital. It's a home. It's our *home*."

"Why didn't you say you were a patient? Wouldn't it have made things much easier?"

I screamed at him. "I am not a patient, Hawkins! You might be a patient but I am not. I am a resident. Got that?" I waited a bit and thought of something else. "And I don't want to make things easier for you, boyo. I want to make them harder. Harder! Understand?"

He hadn't heard me. "You're number seventy-eight. Right at the top. So you manage pretty well. And you think I should too."

I sobbed, "I hate you. I hate you because you needn't be here at all. Because you've had everything you wanted out of life and now there's something you want more than life and you're sulking because you can't have it!"

He went on reflectively, "I think you're the screwball I saw when I arrived. Covered in daisies. I thought the place must be a loony bin."

"Get off this line! I don't want to talk to you ever again—get off this line!"

"All you have to do is to put your phone down."

I put my phone down. It was surprising it didn't shatter into pieces.

7

GRANNY SAID plaintively, "It was steak last night. And I couldn't eat it. I mangled one piece around for half an hour and if I hadn't spat it out I'd have missed dessert too."

"Serves you right." Mr. Pope spoke with great relish. "If you hadn't given your teeth to this young whippersnapper in the first place—"

"You mean if she hadn't been so careless with them! And I reckon she could get the bleeding things back now if she spoke nicely to Staff Nurse Casey."

I said, "You know I won't do that. We're sort of rivals and you don't talk nicely to a rival."

"Balls!" Granny snapped irritably. Hunger obviously made her irritable. Mr. Pope cackled unexpectedly and Granny rounded on him and told him just what she thought of people who nit-picked at their food—fancy ulcer or no fancy ulcer.

We were sitting in the lounge watching the rain sheet down the terrace windows. Tea was still an hour off and lunch seemed years ago. Rosie and I were supposed to be doing a jigsaw puzzle on the coffee table between us, but Rosie had gone to sleep. I wished I had accepted Stella's invitation to swim with the others, but I'd been in the pool in the morning and had the curious sensation that my legs were weighted and were going to drag me to the bottom. Also, I might have caught a cold yesterday in my thin gear; I was shivery and my chest wasn't expanding properly.

Granny came back to me.

"I know why you won't get my teeth back, Miss Termagant. You think you can needle Casey into taking them to Doctor Beamish and reporting you. You think that will be an excuse for them to get together *and* put you in the limelight. Don't you?" Her chin came at me stabbingly. "But that puts *me* in the bloody limelight too, doesn't it? I get cold-shouldered by the nurses. I'm a naughty old lady who's going senile and must be transferred to some geriatric ward at the earliest opportunity."

"I'll get them back for you. Stop worrying." I tried to turn my mind to Casey and Beamish but it was hard. What did Lucas Hawkins look like? Why hadn't he rung me again last night? I tried to forget the long wakeful hours till daylight; the rain on my dormer; Dorothy and Zeek somehow withdrawn from me as I lay with my face turned toward the silent phone.

Had he slept? Had he got some kind of peace from needling me as I had needled him?

"It's over a week. I can't help worrying. I was going to tell them I'd dropped the things down the crapper—"

Mr. Pope yelped, outraged, "The *what?*"

"Crapper. What are you—some kind of nancy boy that you can't understand plain English when it's spoken to you?"

I said, "Don't do that. Casey hasn't found out yet who they belong to. She'll know for sure if you announce you've dropped them down the bog."

"The *bog?*" Mr. Pope tried to look horrified through his enjoyment.

"I should tell her you've taken them. Which is true—almost. When she tells Doc Beamish, I shall say you whipped them—"

"She wouldn't tell Beamish. She'd just give them back to you and smile across at me ever so sweetly—"

"She wouldn't report me?"

"Of course not. Casey is a perfect gentleman."

Granny's mouth practically turned itself inside out. "Then why didn't you say so before? That's what I'll do. I'll ask her for them. Now. Where is she?" She started to get out of her chair, pulling frantically at her Zimmer walking aid.

I restrained her. "You can't do that. It's too tame. At the moment they're a possible weapon. For her and for us."

It was Granny's turn to be outraged. Mr. Pope chortled.

"What are you going on about, girl? Of course

71

they're a weapon. A weapon I use in my battle with food. Only they're no good stuck in—"

"You know what I mean. Calm down. I'll think of something."

"It's been over a week. It was funny at first. I admit it. Not anymore." But she subsided into her chair.

"Look. I'll have them for you by—"

"Tonight," she supplied firmly.

"It's fish tonight. You don't need them for that." I was too tired to think out any plans today. "Tomorrow. I'll get them for you tomorrow. How's that?"

"Lunchtime?" Granny nagged.

"Or dinner." I held up my hand as she half rose. "Tomorrow. I promise." I smiled at her engagingly. "Cool it, baby."

Mr. Pope added sententiously, "If you can't stand the heat keep out of the kitchen."

Granny gave him a malevolent look. "I'm going to get even with you, Arthur Pope," she said.

He looked pleased at the prospect.

I couldn't face tea and went to my room to think. Or rather to face my thoughts, which I knew were unpleasant. First and foremost was my stupid handling of Lucas Hawkins; how was it that from being puppeteer I had suddenly become puppet? Why, when I was smarting and burning up from his realization of my incompleteness as a human being—when I hated his guts in fact—had I waited for him to ring me again last night? Had I honestly expected an apology, or something equally ingratiating? If I had hoped for anything like that, I certainly hadn't got it and I hated him more. One thing was certain. I was not going to ring him again and I was definitely—certainly—one hundred percent positively—not going to fall in with the Beamish/Uncle Roger/Aunt Nell plan to lure him out of his hole with my marmoset attractions.

I shuddered and held the arms of my chair tightly. I didn't want to see him. The thought of seeing him tore me apart. Because he had been allowed to see behind my facade. He knew how very much I hated my incompleteness. How pathetic was my triumph over Casey's spurious "jealousy." Oh God, he knew. He knew me as well as I knew myself. I couldn't ever meet him. It would be like Granny Gorman having to face a mirror all day.

Frantically I tore my thoughts away from that subject and tried to think of a plan to retrieve Granny's teeth without losing any of the edge I had on Casey. I sweated with the effort. I dallied with the idea of stealing them. If they were in Casey's overall pocket maybe I could clutch her around the middle as she got me out of the bath.

I was just picturing a wrestling match on the bathroom floor and trying to summon a grin, when the phone rang.

I nearly fell out of my chair reaching for it; that's how far Lucas Hawkins was from my thoughts.

Stella said, "Mrs. Pountney has got a marvelous idea, Fran. Can you come down?"

I felt so flat it was incredible. My watch was at five

o'clock; another two hours till dinner; I had already spent a fruitless hour thinking and sweating and cringing. Could I face another two? But then could I face Mrs. Pountney and Stella—and doubtless Penny too—and their dedicated enthusiasm?

"No."

She hated flat monosyllables, did Stella. She was so used to sifting and analyzing every damned thing for her O levels that a mere yes or no left her pantingly dissatisfied. It was my way of punishing her for not being Lucas Hawkins.

"Oh *Fran*. Don't be mean. We *need* you. You could make it *go*."

"Make what go?"

"A play. Or an entertainment. Or something. Mrs. Pountney says we could put it on for Fete Day. Oh Fran, *please*. It'll be such fun. Dennis wants to do Peter Pan and be Captain Hook."

"Great." How did they expect me to worry about Granny Gorman's teeth, the nonstart of the Casey-Beamish romance, Lucas Hawkins . . . *plus* a blasted play for Fete Day? Not that Stella realized any of this. And she and Penny were so marvelous with their armless flipper-hands and their unending perseverance. I said wearily, "Give me half an hour. I have to change my pants."

"Okay. But don't be long, Fran. It's nearly time for dinner. I'll be secretary and write everything down, shall I?"

"Sure. You do that." I put the phone down and actually cried at the thought of Stella tortuously taking notes. Then, amazingly, I felt better. I looked around and let my room sink into my consciousness again; the security of it, yet with the rain washing over the dormer like a waterfall, its *beleagueredness*. There was Dorothy lying comfortably on the bed I'd made all by myself before Casey even arrived this morning; there were the flowers, some of them drooping as if under the weight of their own scent; there was Zeek, still smooth and nude inside—that must be remedied soon; there were the wide, shining boards and the low cupboards set under the eaves, and my table laid with scissors and glue and more magazines and . . . everything. It was mine in a way that the wards in previous hospitals could never have been. I had left them without regrets; I had left transitory friends without too many regrets also. It was different now. I had been here a week and two days but there was nothing here I could easily shake off and forget. Everything here had meaning and significance that I didn't even understand yet, but I knew would be revealed to me bit by bit.

"For instance," I said quite loudly to hear myself above the rain. "For instance, that Casey is as soft as butter underneath the enamel." I began to work off my jeans and pants. "And for another instance, that Granny Gorman is still May Gorman inside, who could lead the blokes a fair dance"—I gasped a laugh as I pushed the jumble of clothing from my legs. "And for yet another instance, that Aunt Nell sat up with Timmy Royston all night long. . . ." I hauled clean pants upward and paused, staring down and seeing

75

nothing. I thought of childless Aunt Nell, her anxious blue eyes, the way she had said to Uncle Roger, "We cannot ask Fran." Ask Fran to—what? Ask Fran to help them to help someone. Lucas Hawkins. And because Fran's pride had taken a fall, she'd decided she wasn't going to consider—think—dream—of helping Lucas Hawkins in any way whatsoever.

After a bit I went on dragging the pants up over the objects called knees, rocking from side to side to get them over hips; going through the whole process again with clean jeans; rolling up the castoffs and putting them in my laundry basket; holding Dorothy against my face to cool—or hide—its burning.

There was no escape. I had met Aunt Nell twice and already knew she was my Friend and my friend. She would probably die for me. She was my bulwark. Mine. She was irritating and humorless and completely uncool. And when it was my turn she would sit with me and hold my hand and she wouldn't do it to earn herself a place in heaven. She would do it for love.

Angrily I turned my chair back from Zeek's threshold and snatched up the telephone and dialed five.

As it clicked, I snapped, "Be in the O.T. room in ten minutes flat. And don't get any ideas. I'm doing this for Aunt Nell."

Before I could even make certain it was him on the other end I slapped down the receiver—how long would my phone last with the sort of treatment it was getting? Then I left for the O.T. room myself.

Mrs. Pountney wasn't there. Mrs. Tirrell and the

young chap called Henry and all the kids sat around the worktable. Henry was silent, Mrs. Tirrell trying vainly to quieten the vociferous voices around her. Stella, her nose against her notebooks, was apparently taking notes. In the corner sat Granny, grinning toothlessly. She called out to me as soon as the door opened, "I'm not taking part. But I want to see what you're going to do!"

Her enjoyment, bordering on malicious, spurred me as usual.

"Pity," I said calmly. "You'd be perfect as a wicked witch."

Rosie Jimpson, who had come spinning over to me, diverged to Granny. "Oh go on—please Gran— please. Then I can be Little Red Riding Hood and you can be the wolf. If you can do a witch you can *easily* do a wolf."

Dennis' voice rose above hers. "Captain Hook. I wanna be Captain Hook. Then I can have a sword fight with—"

Henry banged on the table and everyone shut up for a blessed few seconds.

"We'll put it to the vote now Fran's here. Personally I think a concert would be better. Where we all do our particular thing. A song or a recitation perhaps."

Mrs. Tirrell nodded eagerly. Stella rose from her notebook.

"A bit like a competition though," she suggested doubtfully.

Granny snorted. "Boring too. You'll have half the audience crying over you."

77

"We don't want *that*," Penny said definitely. "Whatever we do, let's make them laugh. Please."

She'd put it in a nutshell. Even Rosie and Dennis were willing to make Red Riding Hood and Captain Hook into comic cuts for that reaction. In the end we worked out a loose format; we would all be our favorite pantomime characters, meeting on the stage with some bewilderment and an equal determination to act out our own particular fairy tale. That way we could write our own dialogue and fit it together during rehearsals.

Dubiously we surveyed each other.

"It's not very—er—precise," Mrs. Tirrell mentioned diffidently. "I feel we ought to have a complete story. Otherwise surely it will develop as individual turns without any linking—"

"A band!" I looked around at them, grinning. "We must have a band! We can all be in it—black and white sheets over us to represent evening dress. Then we throw off the sheets—in turn of course—and emerge as our wishful characters. We try to organize the others into playing part of our story. When they get fed up, they play loudly and drown out the performer and—"

"And the next one has a go." Stella looked up, forgetting to write. "That would be perfect. We'd all be on the stage at the same time too—give each other a bit of courage . . ."

Granny leaned forward eagerly. "I can play the tambourine. I was in the Salvation Army years ago and was their star turn."

Mrs. Tirrell smiled yet again. "I can manage 'Three Blind Mice' on the recorder."

"Hey Fran!" Dennis waved his arms to get attention. "I've seen some drums and things in a cupboard in the art room. Let's go and look." He bowled himself down the room eagerly. Everyone was laughing and in good spirits. Someone said it was time for dinner and suggested we have another meeting tomorrow. The rain drummed on the skylights and next door the enormous plastic cover over the swimming pool creaked like ancient ship's timbers in a storm. And there was no sign of Lucas Hawkins.

Dennis yelled, "Come *on*, Fran! I can't see in here, it's nearly dark! Where's the lights?" And I called back, "Not now. Let's look tomorrow before swimming."

There was the usual fuss of wheelchairs queueing up for the door. Granny said to me, "Don't forget what else you're going to do tomorrow, Miss Termagant."

"Okay, okay."

Dennis bawled, "*Fran*—it's dark—"

"Oh for God's sake." I did a three-point turn out of the queue and whizzed down the room and through the swing doors with a crash. "Dennis, come *on*. We can look for some instruments tomorrow!"

It was dark in the art room. Normally it was lit well with enormous skylights, but this evening they seemed underwater, and Dennis groping with a long cane along the top of the store cupboards looked like a small ghost in his white shirt.

79

He said, "They were up here somewhere. I remember when Doreen was dusting she said they should be put away properly."

From the corner of my eye I saw something. For some reason I kept going slowly toward Dennis without turning my head. But I concentrated on the corner of my eye like mad.

"She said they were dust traps. But Mrs. Pountney just gave her some plastic bags for them and told her to—"

A faint movement over by the light switches; stealthy. Someone was making for the other set of doors that led into the changing rooms and then out into the garden. Someone in a chair.

I said, "For Pete's sake, Dennis. Will you come *on!* Right now. I missed tea and I don't intend to miss dinner. And it's fish and chips, which I understand is your favorite." I kept talking, and under cover of my yap the figure, swathed in a rug, I now saw, glided toward those doors.

Dennis was giggling. "Granny won't be able to have any chips, will she? You should have heard her before you came tonight, Fran. She said you were going to use her teeth as a weapon to attack Doctor Beamish with."

"Never end a sentence with a preposition and always get your story straight. Now come on." I turned to my left so I wouldn't have to face the intruder and started back.

Dennis put the cane down. "Yes, but what did she *mean*, Fran? Don't go that way—we can go through the swimming pool and—"

"And get very wet crossing the terrace," I interrupted swiftly. I put on a spurt and opened the swing doors with my step. As Dennis whizzed through I heard the changing-room doors close with a sigh.

Dennis said, "I'd like to go out in the rain. Funny, we're allowed out in the nice weather and we can get wet in the pool, but never in the rain."

I knew what he meant, of course. But it didn't stop me worrying about Lucas Hawkins getting soaked to the skin through his rug. Oh yes. It was Lucas Hawkins who had sneaked in and listened to our plans for an entertainment. I had no doubt about that. And I had been tempted—so tempted—to say casually, "Switch on the lights, would you, Hawkins? They're right by your elbow." But I hadn't. And I didn't know why I hadn't. I hoped very much I hadn't deliberately let him get away with his plan for seeing and not being seen. I mean . . . I didn't want to turn saintly or anything like that.

8

 HE DIDN'T RING that night. Neither did I. The whole question of Lucas Hawkins seemed now to be in abeyance, resting quietly at the back of my mind somewhere, no longer nagging and abrasive; no longer fermenting with excitement; but there—steadily there. He had seen me and I had allowed him to see me. Made myself vulnerable. I couldn't understand why I wasn't raw and quivering— unless it was because I was identifying with Aunt Nell. I was seeing her differently now; as a human being without any defenses to put up. You had to respect people like that. So perhaps I was respecting myself a bit just then.

Of course I'd have been happier if he had rung. Presumably if he didn't ring at all it meant he'd written me off as a nonentity. A mere marmoset. That bit deeply into my ego and I hated it. But I hung on to the fact that I'd done what I could and got him out of his room. I couldn't worry about what happened next.

So we had fish and chips—Granny just had fish—and went to bed on that rainy night and then Casey was bending over me, her cornflower eyes full of concern. Yes, concern.

I mumbled, "Whassup? It's not morning yet."

The concern erased itself. She said briskly, "It's seven thirty. Your bath is ready. You've overslept."

I was surprised; I wasn't a sleeper—quite the opposite. I pushed myself up, put Dorothy on the pillow, let Casey pull my legs around.

"What happened? I didn't even have a pill last night."

"Quiet conscience?" Casey asked snidely. "Come on. Onto your chair."

I put my arms round her waist. Both pockets were empty. Damn. Today was, after all, teeth day.

"Could be," I agreed tranquilly. "How did *you* sleep?"

Did her full mouth twitch? "Fine. As usual." She wheeled me through Zeek and next door to the bathroom. The rain had gone and the tent of my dormer was solid blue sky again. I could change my flowers.

I said, "Have you ever slept with anyone Casey? A man I mean?"

"Dozens." She pulled my nightie over my head, swung my legs into the bath, lowered me after them.

83

She did it so neatly, so expertly. She didn't breathe heavily and neither did I.

"Seriously. Tell me Casey. I need to know—I'm two years older than Juliet and I don't know a thing."

"You probably know a lot more than I do." She left me soaping myself while she lined the bath seat with towels and put lanolin and powder to hand. She couldn't have sounded more uninterested if she'd tried.

"Oh I've read everything. Of course." I tried to keep an eye on her unobviously. "But reading is one thing and knowing is another." She didn't say anything and I had a sudden nasty feeling she might be all buttoned up about it and frigid. That wouldn't do for Beamish at all.

I dunked myself and said briskly, "Of course I can't ever *know*. Not personally. I realize that. But I thought you could tell me . . . something."

She hoisted me onto the bath seat and pulled out the plug. Then she handed me a towel. She didn't say a word.

I rubbed slowly.

"Casey. Just tell me if it's everything the books say it is. Can't you tell me *that*?"

Her laugh was wonderful; I hadn't heard it before. It would lift Beamish over the moon. She wasn't frigid.

She said, "Actually, no I can't, Fran. Sorry. Why don't you try Bennie? She's got a family and she's had two husbands, I believe!"

"She has?" I was almost shoved off course. Not

quite. "But— D'you mean to tell me you've never slept with a man? Honestly?"

"Some girls don't, you know."

"You're a virgin?"

"You make it sound incredible." She had me neatly back into the chair, dressing gown strategically positioned. "I think I should be insulted."

I flung my arms wide and high. "Yippeee!" I caught her wrist as she pushed the chair back through Zeek. "Casey, I'm so glad. It makes it just perfect."

"Makes what perfect?" She turned the chair and eyed me suspiciously. "What are you up to, Fran? I won't have you meddling in my affairs—you know that. Granny Gorman's teeth are one thing; my personal life is quite another."

"You know they're Granny's teeth?" I paused in adjusting my bra. "How long have you known?"

"All the time," she said briskly. "D'you want this T-shirt?"

"No, the sun top. I don't get it. I thought you'd make such a thing of handing them back to her and being awfully smug about it and—"

"Then you don't know me quite as well as you imagined, do you?"

She picked up the laundry basket and went to the door. "Maybe I'm leaving the next move to you. Out of sheer curiosity."

She began to close Zeek behind her. I called desperately, "Casey, what do I have to do to get them back? I already apologized. Do you want me to ask you nicely to give them to Granny?"

I caught a glimpse of shrugging shoulders.

"That's one way. Especially if Granny's getting on your nerves with her nagging. Which I expect she is." The door stayed ajar. "Well?"

I bit my lip. Was there anything else for it? I knew Casey was standing there grinning to herself, thinking she'd won.

"I'm blowed if I will!" I said. After all, I had till dinnertime. I could think of something.

The door closed very gently. Casey obviously thought she too could afford to wait. I had to laugh. And it might have been my imagination but I thought I heard her laughing too. A marvelous sound. *And* she was a virgin.

Miss Hamlin massaged my buttocks with a ferocity that nearly rolled me off the table.

"Can you feel that?" she gasped, pausing and adjusting the cubicle curtain as Dennis' voice was heard outside.

"Not where you're working. It's flattening my boobs though."

She ignored me. "Can you feel this? This? How about this?"

"Yes. Definitely yes. The time before too."

She repeated several sharp smacks. Drew an invisible pencil line across my rump.

"I think—just think—your sensation area is increasing. Maybe only a centimeter."

"Is that possible?" I twisted around to look at her. "You wouldn't kid me, would you?"

"Anything is possible, Fran. Anything." She looked at me with her solid agate eyes willing me to be convinced.

"But I've had this treatment before. Always. Almost."

A slight smile. "Don't worry. I'm not claiming any credit from ten days' work. A cumulative effect . . . I simply don't know. But your record"—she laid her hand on the base of my spine—"shows *there*. And you can feel here—even slightly here—"

"Yes. Yes I can."

"Don't get overoptimistic, child. It might mean nothing."

"Perhaps this is what is waiting for me. Here at Thornton Hall."

"Waiting for you?"

"Ever since I arrived I've sensed something around the corner. I can't explain."

Suddenly her face broke into a smile of pure camaraderie.

"Isn't that the most marvelous feeling? I get it too."

"You do?" Could Miss Hamlin—pale straw hair and green eyes and professional-single-woman status (and she must be past forty so you could add the label old maid)—could she possibly know what I meant?

"Oh yes. Not all the time of course. But I wait for it now. I recognize it." She laughed as she helped me to sit up.

I let her help me dress. "It's just a feeling then? It doesn't mean anything?"

Her pale brows shot up. "Oh it means something,

all right. Surely you've discovered that something exciting is *always* around the corner. We're just lucky we can sense it."

"Little things maybe. Things you make happen yourself." I was thinking of my midnight wander in search of Granny. And my flowers.

"And big things. Things that happen by themselves." She looked at me very seriously as she settled me in my chair. "Trust your feeling, Fran. It's a good one. And it doesn't often let you down."

Then I remembered Beamish's lovely compliment. And Aunt Nell's night-long vigil. I hadn't made them happen. And they weren't little things either.

"Okay." I grinned at her gratefully and felt my face go solemn. "Only . . . only the way I feel sometimes, it might be too much for me. Tremendous."

She didn't try to reassure me; just nodded soberly. "I know what you mean." She remembered her role and changed her tone. "You're not frightened, Fran?"

"No." I shook my head vigorously. "Just tingly. And . . . as if I've got to do something about it; help it along." I shook my head and started to push my way through the curtains. Then paused. "Miss Hamlin. You know Staff Nurse Casey?"

She nodded. "One of our most efficient nurses. A definite gift."

"And gorgeous-looking."

"Oh yes. She reminds me a little of Marilyn Monroe."

Honestly, there was more to Miss Hamlin than met the eye. I nodded eagerly.

"Tell me something. I mean—give me your opinion. Do you think—er—that is— How about Staff Nurse Casey and Doctor Beamish?"

She looked blank for just a moment, then realization dawned. She pursed her lips and nodded judiciously. "You could have something there. Both dedicated, but she might be able to hold him steady now and then. Yes, that is a possibility."

I flung aside the curtains triumphantly. Dennis was on the sculling machine, Rosie was with a nurse beneath the lamp.

"Why if it isn't Captain Hook and Little Red Riding Hood!" They giggled at me. I felt suddenly all-powerful and certain I was on the right track where Casey was concerned. I turned to Miss Hamlin. "Thanks. Thanks for everything. On the strength of your opinion I'm not going to let any more grass grow under my feet."

"Oh dear."

She was still holding the curtain and watching me when I turned at the door to wave. She looked worried. But that was a compliment too. After all, it showed that she thought I might well get things done.

Mrs. Tirrell was with Doc Beamish, so I waited on the terrace. The garden was breathtaking after the rain. Mr. Ottwell was doing something to his tomatoes in the greenhouse. I waved to him but he didn't see me. The unshaded grass on the big lawn steamed gently and the roses dripped dew. I breathed and let it soak into me. I felt good. The cold that had threatened yesterday must have been psychosomatic. I breathed again and my lungs expanded till they touched my ribs. Lovely. Could I feel the tops of my legs, or was that all psychosomatic too after Miss Hamlin's words? I dug my knuckles into my hips and moved downward, pressing hard. Just where did feeling end? I couldn't tell, and my heart was still yammering away with the possibility that it could . . . it might . . . it *could* happen. Perhaps by the time I was three years older than Juliet when she met Romeo, I would know when I was wetting my pants; and then perhaps I could stop.

I breathed again. I needed air.

I looked down and saw my arms. They were long and beautifully curved and already honey colored. I stretched them in front of me and looked at the backs of my hands; then I brought them slowly to my face, palm to palm, prayerfully. After that they moved by themselves, dancing slowly in the sunlight and with great significance, like the hand movements of a Japanese dancer. I watched them with delight. They were leaves, they were butterflies, they were swallows and throbbing larks and spiky starfish. They were frail and then strong, helpless and then very capable. They fluttered like snowflakes in the winter and struck swiftly like the rain on the sea.

I heard Mrs. Tirrell's chair behind me and turned to her with an apologetic smile.

"I'm vain about my hands. I often watch them in a mirror."

Her gentle horse face was drawn down; she had a

hopeless look. But she found a smile for me.

"Not vain, dear. Proud perhaps. You should be proud. They're lovely hands." She cleared her throat and gave her whole attention to the present. "Perhaps you could do something like that in our concert?"

I was very taken with the idea. "We wanted to make them laugh though," I objected. "My hand dancing isn't funny."

"No, it's beautiful. Let's talk about it at tonight's meeting." Her upper lip came over her lower. "Doctor Beamish is free now if you want to see him, Fran."

"Oh thanks." I hesitated, trying to bring my mind to her fully. "Are you okay, Mrs. Tirrell?"

"Yes. Of course. Perfectly." She neighed a laugh and I knew for certain she was about to cry. There was nothing I could do.

Beamish was writing notes when I got to his door.

"Hullo Fran. Come on in. I won't be a moment." His hair was like a Zulu warrior's and his long jaw extended and retracted as he wrote.

I couldn't wait silently.

"What's up with Mrs. Tirrell?"

He looked up, surprised, his round black eyes without deceit.

"Helen Tirrell? She's just been in. Told me the pain was easier. I don't know Fran. What is up?"

"I think she might be crying."

"Oh." He pushed the notes away. The folder was labeled "Helen Tirrell." He said briskly, "I'll have another word in a moment." Which obviously meant it was something private. Between him and her. I smarted for a moment, remembering he hadn't been above suggesting to Uncle Roger and Aunt Nell that I might help with the problem of Lucas Hawkins. Then he said, "What can I do for you, Fran?" And I remembered why I was here. Two birds with one stone. Return Granny's teeth to her without so much as one word to Casey. *And*—much more important—bring Casey and Beamish together to shake their heads over wicked old me. Maybe laugh a little.

So I told him the whole story. Concluding with, "So I've decided to throw myself on your mercy. Give me a black mark—slap my wrist—put me on bread and water. But please tell Casey to give those ghastly choppers back to Granny Gorman and get her off my back!"

I raised pleading, rueful eyes to his face, asking for a laugh, and was surprised to see nothing there.

"Just a minute, Fran." He came around the desk and sat on the corner next to me, frowning slightly. "Have I got this right? You took Mrs. Gorman's teeth for a joke. Nurse Casey took them from you—knowing to whom they belonged—and has withheld them for over a week?"

"Well yes. But it wasn't quite like that of course."

"And during that time Mrs. Gorman has been unable to eat any solid food?"

"Oh yes. She had fish. And almost anything she can mangle around with her gums. But—"

"But no raw fruit, no crusts, no roughage at all in fact." He stood up. "You did right to tell me this, Fran. Thank you. Leave it with me now."

"It was only a joke," I bleated. "You've got it all wrong."

"I understand. Though I hope you don't play many jokes of that kind, Fran." He went ahead of me to the door. "I'll see Nurse Casey and sort it out. You forget the whole matter. I'll also change your nurse for you so there will be no unpleasantness."

"You'll what?" I felt my temper suddenly explode. "My God! For an intelligent man who is supposed to have all this blasted *empathy*, you—you're *stupid!*"

I suppose he went on staring as I belted along the corridor and crashed through the swing doors onto the terrace again. I didn't know and I didn't care. When there were women like Granny Gorman and Casey around, it gave me a pain to have to deal with men like Beamish. And Uncle Roger. And Lucas Hawkins.

Mrs. Tirrell was way over the lawn looking closely at a bed of begonias. I wondered what our clever orthopedic surgeon-cum-psychologist had been saying to *her*.

I tracked Casey down in the head nurse's office, writing in the daybook. A hint of a smile appeared in her blue eyes when I arrived, and it hurt like hell to think I had doubtless mucked up the special relationship we had.

She said, "If you've come to ask me anything—in suitably groveling phrases—save it a moment while I finish this."

She was going to turn her winning into a joke. The whole thing had been a game and she had played along so well. Why couldn't Beamish have *understood?*

I said, "I can't wait. Because in a moment you're going to be sent for by Beamish and I have to go with you because it's all my fault." The phone rang. I said quickly, "I'm sorry, Casey."

She kept level eyes on me while she lifted the receiver and listened and said, "Very well, Doctor. Right away." Then she said, "Save the apologies, Fran. Come on. I want you with me too."

We went along the corridor, past the lounge and dining room, through the door in the stairs that led to the new block. Casey walked so fast I began to think she was deliberately putting me off speaking. Unless she was eager to see Beamish. Which made my heart sink all over again.

The door was closed and she tapped, waited for his voice, opened it and held it for me to follow. I left it open as a line of fast retreat.

He said, "We don't need you Fran. Thank you."

My God, he could be chilling.

Casey's voice was colder still. "I've asked Fran to stay, Doctor. And she wishes to."

He ran his hand through his hair and shrugged. "It was for your sake, Nurse. However. Obviously Fran has told you what this is all about. For her own perverse reasons she took Mrs. Gorman's dentures. The top set. You have seen fit to keep them for over a week, which has forced Mrs. Gorman to eat only slops." He stopped suddenly and a look of faint bewilderment swept his face. He must have been realizing for the first time what a ridiculous storm in a teacup this actually was.

Casey said calmly, "The first part of that statement is true. Frances took Mrs. Gorman's teeth. It was—I understand—a joke in which they both took part. However—" She looked at me and that smile was there again. Incredibly there. "However, the second part is not true. Naturally I removed the teeth from Fran's possession. Naturally I returned them to Mrs. Gorman immediately."

There was a silence. Then I gulped. "You what? You returned them last week? D'you mean to tell me, Casey, you've kept me dangling on a hook all week? You *rotter!*" I snorted a huge laugh and then spluttered, "And as for that Granny Gorman—the old toad—the snake in the grass—"

Beamish said, "Wait a minute. Could someone please tell me what this is all about?" He recombed his hair with spread fingers. "What it's *really* about?"

Casey looked as if butter wouldn't melt in her mouth.

"Mrs. Gorman might not know her teeth are in a beaker in her bathroom with the lower set," she said demurely. "But surely if she is so anxious to use false teeth, she would have fitted her lower set anyway? I think we can safely assume that Mrs. Gorman has been making a fuss about her 'missing' teeth because—like you, Fran—she enjoys making a fuss about something."

That shut me up. And Beamish too. I glanced at him and saw him fitting it all into place. Casey had won. Hands down. Beautifully and without fuss she had scotched Granny, Beamish and me. What a woman. What a wonderful woman.

And then I saw that I had won too. Because here were Casey and Beamish meeting over a pair of false teeth in the most unclinical way possible. Giggles starting burping through my nose.

Beamish's voice trembled slightly. "I'd like to talk to Nurse Casey about you, Fran," he said severely. "If you don't mind."

"Not at all." I choked and reversed smartly through the open door. It closed behind me and I waited. Two seconds later Casey started to laugh. Beamish snuffled, snorted, wheezed. I supposed it was a laugh; maybe he was keeping it down so that he could hear Casey's melody more clearly.

9

 SEVENTEEN DAYS went by. Seventeen days; just like that; apparently wasted.

My cold wasn't psychosomatic at all. The sense of well-being disappeared the night of Casey and Beamish, and the nightmares started. I was in sick bay in an oxygen tent and my legs were so heavy I was drowning in my own tears. People from other hospitals kept appearing, and the boy who had first seen my likeness to a marmoset screamed at me, "Frances Adamson! More like Fanny Adams! That's what you are—nothing—nothing at all! Sweet Fanny Adams! Sweet F.A."

Every now and then they'd go away and there would be Aunt Nell, blue eyes bulging with anxiety, breasts pendulous as she leaned over me.

"You're a bit better, Frances dear. Just a bit."

And I held her hand and wondered if this was it.

I knew Casey and Beamish were around too. My body recognized Casey's efficient touch; my ears heard Beamish's voice giving instructions, and I resigned my physical self to them gratefully. My mental self surfaced at gradually longer intervals to rest on Aunt Nell. She must have left me sometimes; after all, she had to eat and sleep; but whenever I looked she was there, her hand reaching for mine, waiting to take on my fear and petulance and carry it for me.

And once there was someone else with her. Not Uncle Roger. Someone male and in a wheelchair. Someone who said above Aunt Nell's distressed croonings, "Fanny? Sounds Victorian. Distinguished. Like in a Jane Austen novel." I knew the voice was speaking to me and trying to be encouraging. But of course it didn't know that it was more than the name. It didn't know that above everything else I couldn't bear to be nothing. Not me. Not Frances Adamson.

Aunt Nell's comfort was less bracing and more acceptable. "Children are always cruel, Frances dear. Try not to remember things like that." But still the other voice insisted, "Fanny. Fanny. It suits her."

And then the wheelchair wasn't there but Aunt Nell was. And she was right, I was getting better. My back hurt and I could smell myself and I wanted to cry.

Casey said, "Mrs. Parrish, now that Fran is improving, I think you should go back home."

Aunt Nell looked at me. Her face was ravaged, her sweater sagged at the neck and I could see a mole sprouting hairs.

"I'll stay if you want me to, Frances dear."

I turned my head on the pillow. Had I clung to her and wept and thought she was my mother still loving me? Had I made a fool of myself?

I said, "No. Go home. I'm all right. I don't need anyone."

"Oh." She sighed. Relief or regret? I didn't dare catch her eye in case I begged her to stay. She said, "All right dear. I can come tomorrow after all. It's not far."

I didn't answer her. I wondered if I could last till tomorrow without her. I wondered if I could pretend to be worse again so that she would hold me against her mother-smelling sweater and say, "It's all right, dear. I've got you. Everything is all right now."

Later, Casey did some straightening and propped me while I drank. I wasn't even interested about her progress with Beamish. What a fuss it all was. About nothing. I wondered if this was what had been waiting for me at Thornton Hall. I laughed weakly.

"What's funny, Fran?"

"There's always something waiting for you around the corner, isn't there?" I whispered. "Even if it's only pneumonia."

She settled me gently. "Another day or two and you'll be back to normal," she said and turned down her mouth at the prospect. I looked away. No one was going to inveigle me into being involved again.

But then I was back in my room and the campaign to reintegrate me started. Beamish thought a quick dip in the pool would help enormously. He pursed his mouth when I shook my head, and said, "I'll give you another week of this self-imposed solitary confinement, Fran, then I shall carry you down to Miss Hamlin and afterward take great pleasure in throwing you into the water."

I couldn't summon a smile.

Stella and Penny came up for a chat. They wondered if they could help me write my part for the play. I couldn't remember what they were on about. It was years since our last meeting. Surely all that nonsense was over and done with. No. It was only the first week in July—another three weeks at least to go. I said listlessly, "Tons of time then."

Stella looked at Penny and they began on the absolute impossibility of getting their O levels. But if by any chance passing miracle they did, then they thought they'd have a go at Advanced. What did I think about that? I looked through my dormer at the heartless blue sky that would still be there when Penny and Stella were doing A levels. And when I was nothing. Sweet nothing. When I looked back, they'd gone.

Casey brought Granny in a wheelchair, grumbling about anyone making her come all this way when it would be so much easier for anyone to come down to the lounge for a quiet chat. She gave me a list of menus for the past two weeks, then a list of Mr. Pope's reactions to them. Frowning and muttering even more fiercely, she left after half an hour.

It was the seventeenth day. In the morning Casey said, "It's seventeen days since you were ill. Don't you think you could make a bit of an effort today Fran? How about coming down for lunch?"

"No thanks."

"Tea then? Cook has made some gorgeous cake."

"No thanks."

She snapped abrasively, "Get on with it then. It's known as self-pity." She waited. I didn't rise. Her voice still tart, she added, "You want to be alone, is that it? You want your lunch sent up? Tea sent up? Supper sent up? No visitors? Is that what you want?"

I said, "That's what I want. If you could arrange it."

She crouched and looked at me hopefully. I let my eyes slide off hers and toward the dormer again. She sighed, stood up and left.

I sat there and set myself to thinking of nothing. They say it's not possible. Okay, so it's not, but it is possible to think of a stone. A stone sitting on a lot of land—say a desert. A dreary gray stone, nothing underneath it, no especially interesting shape. Then, when the stone gets boring, switch quickly to a lump of coal. Maybe a mound of coal like you see sitting in railway yards. Count a few of the lumps. Go back to the stone. . . .

You can use up whole half hours without having to resort to a book or a thought. I used up the morning and the lunch hour and some time after, and I got quite a kick out of it. You know, like some people with too much money get a kick out of burning fivers or standing on a bridge and ripping them up and

101

letting them flutter into the water beneath. That's what I was doing with my time. I'd got a limited amount. Why the hell should I try to fill it anymore? A pointless exercise. I would waste it. I was damned well not going to *use* it.

So there I was, Zeek still unfinished, Dorothy lying on her back with a hole in her tummy indecently exposed, my flowers all gone and my room pristine because I'd had to have the cleaners.

And the phone rang.

"Hullo."

"Ah. So you're answering at last. Miss Fanny Adams I presume?"

I thought I'd forgotten him. I thought I'd forgotten our fencing match. And I certainly hadn't realized until then that it was he who had sat by Aunt Nell and heard my ramblings.

"Cheerio," I said and replaced my receiver. But I was smarting. Otherwise I wouldn't have picked it up when it rang again.

"I want to know why you didn't answer yesterday. And the day before. And the day before that. And—"

"It didn't ring. Maybe I was disconnected to save me taking calls from weirdos."

"Very wise. Listen, I kept an eye on things while you were out. Casey and Beamish walked in the garden on Wednesday last. From eight P.M. until eight forty-five."

"Big deal."

"Well, you started it. The least you can do is take a little interest."

"I'll let you do that. Cheerio."

"Fanny—don't go. I want to tell you something—"

"*Don't* call me Fanny! D'you hear me? My name is not Fanny!"

His voice became silky. "Where's your sense of humor? Besides, it suits you. Fanny Adams."

Tears choked my throat. "You think I'm nothing—I know that. You thought Casey and Beamish . . . A lot of fuss about nothing—I know all that—"

He said, "Shut up. Before you say something you wish you hadn't. I didn't ring to sympathize. Nor incidentally to tell you about your matchmaking progress. Something quite different."

"Oh." I swallowed my tears.

"Are you going to listen?"

"Don't know."

"Fair enough. Let's have a go. This concert thing you're doing for Fete Day. It's corny."

I pushed my mind back through fuddled time to the last meeting. Mrs. Tirrell had sat silently throughout the proceedings; Henry had done nothing but keep order between Rosie and Dennis; Granny hadn't stopped cackling, though whether at the meeting or whether with pleasure at regaining her teeth and my discomfiture, I couldn't guess. Dennis had persuaded Mrs. Pountney to unearth a couple of side drums and four triangles, and the noise really had been terrible. I'd sat there and let it drift over me; my head had been aching and I'd had trouble breathing.

I said, "So you came to that meeting too, did you?"

There was a slight pause. Then he said, "You know.

103

You knew I was in the art room. Why didn't you say something?"

"You didn't want to be discovered."

Another pause, longer. He cleared his throat, nearly bursting my eardrum.

"Seems I've got a lot to thank you for, Fanny."

"Don't call me—"

"I'm going to. So get used to it. Thanks, Fanny."

I exploded with a kind of resignation. "Oh . . . *shit!*"

Because it was no good. I couldn't think of stones and coal anymore. Life just would not leave me alone.

He was laughing. "That's better. Now perhaps you'll listen properly. The concert." I said a very rude word about the concert and he went on tranquilly, "Quite. But you can't give up on it now. And the ideas aren't bad. It's just that . . . it'll be so static. A load of wheelchairs maneuvering slowly around while Dennis brandishes his sword."

"What do you suggest?" The sun was shining. I noticed the sun was shining. "Exactly what do you suggest, genius? I wanted to be Peter Pan and fly, but Mrs. Pountney put her foot down."

"Naturally. So where is the place you can all move without chairs? Fast and easily?" My mind was a complete blank and felt sluggish as well. He said exasperatedly, "Come on, Fanny! The pool! Water! You all swim, and the light in there is interesting. You've got the changing rooms right behind—quite enough space at the end and sides for seating—you can have loads of comedy pushing each other in—"

104

"How do you know we can all swim? Have you been spying there too?"

"I've *watched* a couple of times—"

"I call it spying. And you spied on me when I was in sick bay."

His voice was suddenly suffocated. "I don't want to be seen. I mustn't be seen."

"The nurses see you. Aunt Nell."

"They're different. It's their job."

"It's not Aunt Nell's job."

"She was wrapped up in you. I don't think she *saw* me."

I breathed twice. "But even if she had . . . you had to risk that if you wanted to see me," I said slowly.

He didn't speak for ages. At last in an off-hand voice he said, "I thought you might die or something stupid."

My heart beat hard and certain under my nightie. It was three o'clock in the afternoon. What the hell was I doing in my nightie?

I said quietly, "Hawkins. You're a nit. You don't have to spy on *us*. We're all handicapped. Granny can walk with her Zimmer but she's buckling up with arthritis."

Another long silence. I wondered whether he wasn't going to say anything else and my mind searched around for something to *make* him talk about it. Because this was important. I couldn't really remember why it was important, but I knew it was.

His voice came across the line, subdued, cracked. "Oh God, Fanny. I'll never get used to it."

105

I could have melted with pity. I said hardily, "You've had time. A month. And God knows how long before you came to Thornton Hall. I've had pneumonia for seventeen days and they're nagging me to get out and about again. And you've had a month." I counted three and said sensibly, "Now. When's the next meeting about the concert? Come to that. Tell them about your idea. It'll break the ice—"

"No!" It was a shout. He calmed down audibly. "Listen. Try to understand. Supposing . . ." His voice quietened right down and I pressed the receiver hard against my ear. "Supposing you had an accident. Lost your hands."

"My *hands*?"

"Your hands. They're lovely. They talk for you. You use them all the time without knowing it. Supposing you lost them."

I was absolutely silent trying not to imagine it, trying to push the unspeakable thought from me.

He said, "You see, Fanny? That's how it is for me. I played football and tennis. Swam—"

"You could still swim," I said quickly.

"What? You must be joking. I'd upend like a bleeding duck and plummet to the bottom. Charming."

"Oh *Hawkins*—"

"Luke. Call me Luke."

"It's a nancy name. Hawkins, don't you realize that it's in the water you learn to balance? You've *got* to come into the pool. You've got to stop being ashamed. Okay, I'd hate to lose my hands, not only because I'd have to do things like Stella does—and Penny—

but because I'm vain about them. Is that why you won't show yourself? Is it vanity?"

"Look. Shit to that, Fanny. Don't start trying to needle me into the open. It'll be the end of our beautiful friendship if you do."

"Beautiful friendship? Is this what you call a beautiful friendship?" I made my voice as dry as dust because there was desperation zinging across the wires.

He cooled it. "I heard about the teeth, Fanny. Very funny. As it turned out. But supposing Casey hadn't put them in Mrs. Gorman's bathroom?" He snorted an attempt at a laugh. "I'd rather not be the object of one of your crusades."

"She'd have got a reprimand. That's all."

"You said she had a yen for Beamish. So the reprimand would have hurt, yes? She might well have left, wouldn't you say?" He sighed. "Come on, Fanny, use your imagination. You could have cocked everything up well and truly."

"But I didn't. It worked out beautifully."

"I'd prefer not to take any similar risks. So hands off. Okay?"

I nodded as I said, "Okay." But my mind was already working on the problem of getting Hawkins into the open.

He knew. He said, "I *mean* it. If you don't leave me strictly alone, I'll never phone you again."

"And I couldn't stand that," I said with heavy sarcasm.

"No, I know. You've spent a lot of time waiting

for your phone to ring. I wouldn't like to think you had to do that again."

My eyes stretched wide. "What d'you mean? I was the one who rang you, remember!"

"Not always, hey? Not the night of the storm for instance."

"How did you know—" I cut my words off short but he was there.

"I wasn't sure. You just confirmed it."

"You are a rat, Hawkins," I told him levelly. "You are a sadistic rat."

"Listen, Fanny Adams, you'd kept me waiting before then. I was getting so I couldn't take my eyes off the phone."

"Good-bye, rat."

"Good-bye, Fanny. And it *is* a beautiful friendship, so don't wreck it."

The line went dead. I replaced my receiver and stared at it for a long time. Casey came in to see what I'd like for tea. I said, "I'll get dressed and come downstairs. Then I can make up my mind about the cake."

She checked herself on a double take and said dourly, "I knew it wouldn't be much longer."

I was busy with my pants. "Count your blessings, Casey. You've had seventeen days. If you haven't got very far in that time you *need* me."

"Not in that way." She knelt and held out my jeans. "But the place is dull without you. I'll give you that."

Her face was like a flower framed in golden hair and white cap. I grinned at it. "I love you, Casey."

She tightened her full mouth and flipped the jeans expertly up my legs. Maybe she thought I was going soft.

I said insidiously, "Did you enjoy your walk with Doctor Beamish? I do hope no one saw you. You know how quickly rumors spread in a place like this."

She stood up abruptly and grabbed my nightie. She wasn't going to be drawn, though. I decided to go no further. But whole new prospects were opening out. And the biggest one of all was Lucas Hawkins. And how to force him out of his shell.

10

 MRS. TIRRELL SAID, "It's a very good idea, Fran. Exciting. But will you be allowed in the pool so soon? Fete Day is only three weeks away now."

We were in the O.T. room. She had her embroidery frame in front of her, but not much had been done since I saw it last. Granny was knitting; I was cleaning the triangles with Silvo. The others were at school, but I'd told them about Hawkins' idea to turn our concert into an aqua show and they thought it was great.

"Sure," I answered Mrs. Tirrell. "Miss Hamlin says it will help my breathing and—"

"Rubbish," Granny commented. "Hot poultices on your chest. That's what you need, my girl. If I had you in my care you'd be out and about in three weeks all right."

"I am out and about Gran. And it's less than three weeks since I got ill."

"Everyone's swimming mad these days," Granny went on, dropping two stitches. "Too much water isn't good for a body."

Mrs. Tirrell explained sotto voce, "Of course Mrs. Gorman doesn't swim, so she's probably feeling left out."

"*You* don't have to get wet," I told Granny kindly. "You can be the one who pushes us in. Just tip our chairs up and—"

"I have no intention of getting wet, Miss Termagant!" snapped Granny. "And as for tipping your chairs with my arthritis—"

"You'll manage it all right with Mr. Pope's help."

"Arthur Pope? You'll never get him into this!"

"I've already seen him. And he agreed."

I didn't bother to tell her he'd only agreed when I informed him that Granny couldn't cope on her own and had asked for his help.

"He did?" She sucked in her mouth consideringly. "Oh . . . well . . ."

I went on rubbing at the triangle, well satisfied. I had decided during teatime the day before to broach this subject with small groups. The kids were no problem, but the older ones seemed to think it was their duty to object to everything for the first five minutes. Mr. Pope had been a pushover; he really did fancy Gran. Henry was doubtful. Mrs. Tirrell and Granny

111

were fast talking themselves into it while I edged away for a word with Mrs. Pountney.

She frowned. I smiled.

"I'm not keen on the sound of all this falling off the edge," she said. "If the chairs aren't in exactly the right place, either the whole lot goes in or the occupant will fall onto the concrete. It's not safe, Fran."

I bit my lip. Hawkins' idea had to work. "What if some of the O.T. helpers came along? I wanted it to be just us, but—"

"Well . . ." Wasn't she capable of giving an *inch*? "We could try it, I suppose." She patted my shoulder. "They could dress up, Fran—how about a bevy of witches? Mrs. Gorman and Mr. Pope could be their leaders or something?"

It was better than nothing. Much better than nothing.

"Yes. I guess so. Thanks, Mrs. Pountney. We'll start practicing on that tomorrow."

I left her before she could think of other snags. I could see she wished she hadn't gone that far. But she had.

I rang Hawkins during the rest period after lunch.

"Can you get out a script by tomorrow?" I asked without preliminaries. "Mrs. Tirrell wants to be the old woman who lived in a shoe. Henry, Robin Hood. Penny and Stella, the Babes in the Wood."

"Hang on, hang on." He sounded wary. "Let me get pen and paper."

"Are you okay? Shall I ring later?"

"Hey! Consideration from Fanny Adams? I must

112

sound like death itself." He was reviving.

I said, "Yes, you do. And we don't want a rotten script, do we?"

"Oh no. Of course not. We mustn't risk that whatever we do. Anyway I can't write scripts. I've never done it in my life."

"Have you got anything else pressing at the moment? No? Then it looks like now is the time to start writing scripts. Got the pen?"

"Look, I gave you the lousy idea. Can't you do anything for yourself?"

"I can organize people. And I'm organizing like mad. So write down—Frances Adamson, Peter Pan."

"What!" He was outraged. "I only thought of the bloody aqua idea so that you could be the Lorelei!"

I'd opened my mouth to reply before he finished. Now I closed it again. Then I took a long breath.

"How did you know about the Lorelei? Casey. Casey told you. You've been spying in more ways than one, Hawkins. I don't like it."

I could hear laughter in his voice. "I know. It's pretty low, isn't it? Something you wouldn't stoop to. And I'll tell you something for free, Fanny. I didn't have to ask her. She told me."

"Casey wouldn't. She's not like that."

"I got that impression. About most things. But not when it comes to you. I know things about you you don't know yourself."

"Oh—" I was going to come out with some expletive that would make him laugh properly, but I didn't. I suddenly realized why Casey was acting so uncharacteristically. Beamish had roped her into the plan for

113

getting Hawkins out of his hole. Socializing him. Integrating him. Call it what you like. But *I* didn't like it. Not now. Strange, that—I'd been tickled pink at first, then cringing because he'd seen through me, and now . . . now I wanted him to come out, all right. But not for them. Not because of them. For me. Because of me.

He said, "Fanny? You still there?"

"Yeah. I'm here. I don't like it, Hawkins."

"What? Casey doing to you what you did to her?" He snorted a laugh. "Surely you can see why? If I get interested enough in the crazy girl in seventy-eight who fills her room with flowers and whips old lady's dentures, I'm going to want to meet her. I'm going to come out of my room and into the lounge. Where I can be Got At."

"Oh well. If you see through it. I suppose it's okay."

His clear summing-up brought it into perspective. It was still private because it was our joke.

I said, "You wouldn't let yourself be fooled by such an obvious ploy, huh?"

"You told me you were interesting long before Casey mentioned it. And anyway I've seen for myself. Four times."

The conversation was now fascinating. "Tell me exactly when and where. The art room of course. And when I was ill. What about the other two times?"

"I can't remember," he said airily. "It's not important, is it?"

I ground my teeth. "Not at all. Uh . . . but you saw what I meant, I suppose?"

"Meant?"

"You know. About me being interesting."

"I can't honestly recall my exact impressions at the time."

I could hear him laughing silently. I said, "I hate you, Hawkins. You do *know* that? You're quite *clear* about that?"

"Sure," he said equably. "Now. Skirmish over. I'll write a script so long as you don't quibble. About anything."

"Umm. Well. Okay. Up to a point. Nothing top-less."

"Mermaids are always topless, Fanny. I realize you're an ignoramus but surely you know that?"

"If you can sell it to Mrs. Pountney I'll do it. And I'm not an ignoramus. Just because I won't go to school anymore doesn't mean I don't know anything. I know more than most people."

"Tell me about Nietzsche."

"Oh for Pete's sake—"

"Thomas Aquinas?"

"Look here, Hawkins—"

"Dylan Thomas? The Romantic poets? Othello? The Wife of Bath?"

"Yes—yes, I know about them! I do! I love the Green Fuse and I hate Iago and the Wife of Bath is just my cup of tea. So there."

I heard him sigh. "One sentence. One little sentence plus a colloquialism dismisses a range of great English writers—"

"Oh shut up. If you want a thesis, come back in a year's time."

"Okay. Will do. Start now. Limit yourself to one

115

of them—Dylan Thomas I'd guess. Read everything he ever wrote. A couple of biographies—reviews, obituaries, everything like that. But *get started.*"

I said slowly, "Beamish has been talking to you too. About my education. My God."

He laughed across the wires, then said briskly, "I haven't got time to talk to you now. There's a play to write before bedtime. Good-bye."

He got his phone down a split second before I did. On the whole I was the loser of that encounter. Though on the other hand, he *was* going to write a script. So already he was part of the concert, however much he protested.

I'd never been in the library. Mrs. Tirrell was there, half a dozen books spread out on the center table. She looked up with a smile, but her velvet-brown eyes were softly mournful as usual.

"Fran. How nice. But you should be resting, shouldn't you? You were up all morning."

"I'm full of energy again. I think I've been well for almost a week but I wouldn't admit it."

The library was original. The Thornton kids must have studied here. Maybe climbed the shelves like ladders and stacked the dusty old tomes into walls and houses. Maybe read. I liked the paneling and the smell of books and the molded ceiling and the different view from the windows. We were at the front of the Hall.

I ran my chair alongside Mrs. Tirrell's. Her books were large illustrated ones; fairy tales, nursery rhymes. I grinned.

"You're getting cracking."

She pushed the nearest book away diffidently. "Well . . . I'm the oldest and I feel the least I can do . . . Besides, it takes me out of myself."

I grinned. "You're not older than Granny, are you?"

"You know what I mean. I feel I should take some responsi*bility*. I'm not very good at that. Even if I could still move around—" She grimaced horribly at her chair. "Even then I think I'd be a background sort of a person."

I narrowed my eyes at her comically. "Yes. I think you would too. You'd be one of those women with a lot of hidden power." I giggled. "The woman behind the man."

She tried to laugh and drew the nearest book onto her lap as an indication that the conversation was concluding.

"You're no good as a character reader, Fran. Even before the accident I was never that."

"Accident? I didn't know you'd been in an accident." I'd thought Hawkins was our only accident case. Was there some help here for him?

She smiled an affirmative and pretended to read.

I said, not very tentatively, "I suppose that's worse? You can compare and remember. Yes, it must be worse."

She glanced up and said brightly, "Not really. I expect it's the same for all of us." She turned a page. I began to feel thankful for Hawkins' anger. It was better than this.

I borrowed his tone and his words. "Of course it's

117

not. *We* don't know what it's like to walk and run and dance."

She lifted her eyes from the book, surprised for a moment. Then she said calmly, "I think the world is divided into two kinds of people, Fran. Strong ones—masters of fate—and victims. If you're a victim then you're always one. Obviously I'm a victim now—of a tragic car accident. But I was one before. So the difference is not very great."

I stared at her, almost fascinated by her complete objectivity and the different picture she was painting from the one I'd got of her in my mental file. When Aunt Nell came, there was always a visitor for Mrs. Tirrell. Mr. Tirrell. He came in a large car and took her out and kissed her on her forehead when he left and held both her hands in his and brought her flowers and fruit. She had obviously been good and loved and horsy all her life. Done petit point and good works. What was all this about being a victim?

She went back to her book. I said, "Can you explain a little more? I don't understand."

She looked at me, still indulgent, and closed the book on her lap.

"About being one of life's victims?" She tried to make it sound funny and her long face became horribly roguish. "What is there to understand about that? It just happens."

I said persistently, "How did it happen to *you*? I want to know about you, Mrs. Tirrell. Did your mother—" I cleared my throat self-consciously. "Did your mother reject you or something?"

The indulgent roguishness disappeared. She thought about it.

"Yes. Perhaps she did," she said consideringly. "In a way."

I was triumphant. "Well, then I would understand, Mrs. Tirrell. Surely you know that my mother left me on a doorstep sixteen years ago?"

She stared at me and soaked that up. She hadn't known obviously. You could see her assimilating and accommodating the fact of me All Alone. No known father or relative. Me, sitting on a pinnacle, doubtless made of ice, in the midst of nothing.

I brought her back to the subject in hand.

"So why are you a victim and not me, Mrs. Tirrell? It doesn't make sense."

She blinked and repeated, "It just happens. To some people." Then her eyes became unfocused and she looked past me. "I don't know. I really don't know. Things happen and you begin to *believe* in your ill luck." Her eyes were glazed. "It must be more than that. But I don't know.

I glanced around in the direction of her gaze. Through the window, the porticoed front door jutted into our line of vision and the long drive began its sweep around to the gates. She wasn't seeing them. Maybe she thought I was seeing what she was seeing, because as I stared through the window, she started up again as if we were both watching a film roll by.

"I suppose my father loved me." Her voice was blankly hopeless. "I remember him vaguely. Sitting me on his knee and saying that beauty was in the eye of the beholder." She smiled slightly without a trace of bitterness. "I must have been such a disappointment to them. I wasn't a boy. Yet I looked like one. And I acted like a Victorian miss." She breathed a laugh and then was silent again. I stayed rigidly still; from the edge of my left eye I could see her, still and staring. A martyr.

"Mother was kind enough when he died." The hopeless voice held the slightest trace of . . . amusement? "But she was always distant. Very distant. Father sometimes called me Nell, but Mother always used Helen. Even when I looked after her during that last frightful illness she was the same. But brave. Very brave." She sighed sharply; she had a high goal to live up to. "And then I was on my own with a house and an income. And thirty years of the wrong kind of experiences behind me. I'd never worked—not a job, I mean. When the Mathiesons took me up—dinner every Tuesday, tennis parties in the summer, bridge in the winter—I was so grateful. They were the only ones. All the old neighbors . . . nobody else . . . socially I was no good you see. Heavy in the hand. And a woman on her own at a dinner party . . . I don't blame them." She relaxed slightly. "Yes, the Mathiesons were kind. It wasn't their fault that Eric was there for the weekend when I called. They were out and he asked me to give him a game of tennis. . . ." She tensed up again. "I was the perfect partner. Always available. I'd run myself off my feet to give him a decent game. But I'd never win. Well, once or twice, when he let me." She laughed. Unpleasantly. "I can't blame him for wiping his feet all over me. I made myself a doormat, after all."

So. She didn't blame anyone. Fine. Just fine. Or was it? I could always blame my mother. My unknown, invisible mother. For the first time in my life I appreciated my mother.

She wasn't going to say any more. She was fingering the plastic cover of her book. A ragged end caught her nail and she pushed at it. It made an agonizing sound. My own nails ached.

I coughed. In for a penny, in for a pound.

"Eric . . . is that Mr. Tirrell?"

She brought her eyes away from the window and looked at me as if I'd sprung out of the paneling. I smiled. As daft as the dogs.

"Oh. Yes. Eric Tirrell. Yes, he is my husband." She pulled at the plastic cover.

"And you got married. That was nice. Then you had your accident."

"That's right." She saw me waiting and said brightly, "In his new Aston Martin. We toured for our honeymoon, you see. In his Aston Martin." She stared down at the book. "I remember thinking—as we coasted down that long hill into Lynmouth about midnight—I remember thinking if it hadn't been for the baby I would be content to die right then." She stripped a piece of plastic completely away and it fell to the floor. "I suppose it was about two seconds later that we left the road."

There was a very long silence. I put it together like a jigsaw puzzle. It came out clearly. Eric Tirrell

121

had had to marry Helen whatever. She had been pregnant. And she had lost her baby along with the use of her legs.

I said at last, "Mrs. Tirrell. I'm sorry. I shouldn't have asked you. I'm sorry."

She looked at me again; gave that horrible bright smile. "Oh, don't worry Fran. Like I said, there's not much difference between you and me. Except that you rise above your . . . legs—" She gave a ghastly giggle. "The really funny part is that Eric is also a victim now. He thought it was his fault, you see, so he couldn't go off and start again with someone else. He has to stick by me. I relieved him of my presence by paying to come here, but he still visits me every weekend—brings me flowers . . ."

I said hoarsely, "I know—I've seen him." I coughed myself clear. "Mrs. Tirrell, you mustn't feel sad for him. He likes coming to see you—he wouldn't come if—"

"Sad? For Eric?" She smiled at me forgivingly. "I knew you wouldn't understand, Fran. I'm not sad for my husband."

I wanted to say "Poor Eric" but stopped myself. Instead I said, "Why are you so sad then? Oh I know . . . your legs and the baby . . . but your sadness is always *there.* You were crying the other day. After you'd seen Doctor Beamish."

"Oh that?" Her upper lip came over her lower. "Yes. Well, he wants me to go back home, Fran. He thinks that's my place. Eric had been to see him. . . . Douglas doesn't realize that Eric is motivated by guilt, you see."

122

"Are you in love with Doctor Beamish?"

Immediately after I'd said it I wished I hadn't. It was like touching a snail's horn. She flinched and cringed all in one. And she was gone from me. Probably for always.

I said again, "I'm sorry Mrs. Tirrell. I shouldn't have said that. I've got used to being cheeky to Granny and . . . I shouldn't have said it."

She took a couple of seconds to recover, then she got that awful smile out again and said, "That's all right, Fran. I remember at your age all I could think about was falling in love."

I played along with her. "I think I'm a bit in love with him myself." I sighed dramatically. "Anyway, thanks for talking to me. It's one of the things I like about Thornton Hall. Being treated as an adult."

"Well, you're grown up now, dear. And so full of life and ideas. Which reminds me—" She looked down at the book again. "Oh dear, I seem to have torn this somehow."

She began to smooth the plastic back into place. I moved away to search for something about Dylan Thomas. I felt sad.

Granny was a surprisingly unwilling recipient of my steak at dinner that night.

"You've got a lot of ground to make up, Miss Termagant. Come along now—cut it up small and try."

"I can't eat it. Honestly, Gran. I'll have your ice cream if you like."

"I'd forgotten how you two swap your meals," Mr. Pope said. "It's disgusting."

123

"There's no pleasure when she's giving it away," Granny grumbled. "It's just my luck to sit at a table with a pair of nit-pickers like you two."

Mr. Pope said, "I notice you don't move elsewhere."

"Neither do you," Granny came back belligerently. She turned to me. "Three weeks he's been carrying on about the way I enjoy my food. And he's still here. Still grumbling."

"Hark who's talking," Mr. Pope remarked bitterly. "She never stops. If I eat something then I'm not doing myself any good. If I don't—"

"Nit-picker." Granny was reduced to name-calling as she came to grips with the steak. "Moaning minnie."

I raised my brows at Mr. Pope. "I told you she fancied you. I can see I'm coming between you two. Excuse me."

Granny tried to catch my arm; bleated, "Fran, you haven't had the ice cream."

But I grinned over my shoulder. Bennie would be up at ten with coffee and custard creams and there were two hours of daylight before then. I wanted to pick the flowers as they closed for the night and sit on the horseshoe lawn and make a daisy chain. For the first time in my life I was consciously grateful for what I had. As Mrs. Tirrell said, I was not a victim. Most of the time I was up there on top. I wanted to be by myself and relish that. And watch my hands move in the evening sunlight.

11

 WHEN BENNIE CAME up to tuck me in I asked her about Hawkins. She said he'd had a bad day but had been writing letters all the time so had been doing his best to "throw it off."

"He's improving—his attitude is better," she said as she stirred extra sugar into my coffee. Casey would have a fit—not so much at the extra sugar but at the way Bennie waited on me. "He's been out of his room once. To meet Mrs. Parrish. It was when you were ill."

So that was his story, was it? And his scriptwriting was also covered up.

"He's very stubborn," she went on. "Still won't see his parents or try to use crutches. As for artificial legs—"

I sipped my syrupy drink appreciatively. "I can't understand why he agreed to come here. I mean, if he doesn't intend to make use of the facilities, he might as well have stayed in hospital until he could face his home again."

Bennie got Aunt Nell's earnest look. "He'd heard about Thornton Hall. I think he might have visited here with his school three or four years ago. You know, like they do now. Anyway he knew he would have his own room and that if he didn't want to come out of it he wouldn't be coerced."

"I see. And he's only been out once."

"Well . . ." Bennie smiled as she opened my bed and gathered cups and plates onto a tray. "Once when I went in with his dinner, he wasn't there. He told me he'd been in the bathroom, but his rug and dressing gown were wet, as if he'd been out in the rain. I didn't say a word."

"Good old Bennie. By the way, is that window in the lounge always unlocked?"

"Now Fran! You've already been in the garden once this evening and it's dark now."

"I was simply asking in case you're not on duty sometime when I need fresh air."

"I see." She tightened her lips at me. "It's usually just latched so that we can let the dogs in and out when necessary."

"Good old Bennie," I repeated. I smiled my marmoset smile at her and she touched my hair as she went past. Very occasionally it was rather nice when someone thought you were marvelous. Just because you couldn't walk.

126

* * *

I couldn't wait to see if he'd ring me. Pride or no pride, I dialed number five soon after eleven, when I knew Bennie would have gone to the staff room for a couple of hours. He was surprised and still weary. Much wearier than he'd sounded that afternoon. Of course he'd written a script since then.

I said, "I've been out in the garden this evening. First time for ages. It was marvelous. Lots of changes. There are red-hot pokers in the lavender hedge. And a new crop of pansies. Brown with yellow blotches. Like butterflies."

He said, "You're really better. I'm glad. Fanny, I've got to ring off. If I don't sleep I'll go mad."

"Have they given you sleeping pills?"

"Yes. They're here. I didn't want to take them till I'd phoned you. And that's supposed to be at midnight. I thought."

"Rules are for breaking. Listen Hawkins, don't take them. You won't need them if you go for a stroll in the garden. Honestly. I guarantee you a full night's sleep if you follow these directions absolutely."

"Don't be a fool. The place is locked up. The dogs would let fly."

"That's really funny. My second night here I did a midnight ramble and didn't even see them. That was when I found out the number of your room. Also the French door in the lounge is on the latch. The lounge is opposite the staircase."

"Fanny . . . I can't."

"It's not fair, Hawkins. You've seen me and I haven't seen you."

127

"My stumps are aching to glory, Fanny."

"Don't give me that crap. You know you need fresh air. You're scared. That's your trouble. You're scared."

"Dammit all, what do you want from me, girl? I've gone along with these crazy phone calls. I've spent the whole afternoon and half the night getting something down on paper for your lousy concert—"

"I'm leaving right now Hawkins. I'll wait for you half an hour on the horseshoe lawn. Where you saw me when you arrived. If you haven't come by then, don't bother to phone again."

I put the phone down. My God, what had I done? The moths beat feebly against the dome of my dormer, trying to reach the light. I stared at them knowing how they felt. Whether Hawkins came or not made no difference. There was no future for people like me.

I left the window wide for him, praying the dogs wouldn't ask to be let out before my return. My wheels made no sound on the flagged terrace, and I coasted down the ramp and straight over the gravel path onto the grass. The small crunch as I crossed the loose stones was minimal. I was almost certain the open ground-floor windows along this side of the house belonged to Granny, Mr. Pope and the other adults. Dennis, Rosie, Stella and Penny were grouped around the nurses' quarter. I realized again how lucky I was to have my room upstairs with its isolated privacy.

There was no moon as yet, but the night was light

with stars. Anyone taller than the lavender and box hedges would be completely visible, so that made me all right. There must have been quite a bit of rain while I'd been ill, because my wheels had to be shoved every inch over the turf, but I didn't mind. The night air was sharply chill and I needed to keep warm. Belatedly I wondered whether it would be good for Hawkins to be out here after so long indoors.

It was a bit dicey crossing the wide-open space of the horseshoe lawn. I felt hideously exposed, and it was as if my wheels were plowing through mud, they were so sluggish. I made for the whispering aspen where I'd sat when Aunt Nell and Uncle Roger had first suggested that I might help to "integrate" Lucas Hawkins. It seemed appropriate to wait for him there. Besides which, I could then survey the unshadowed approaches and go to meet him if—*when*—he came.

Then I waited.

There were a lot of sounds. The aspen trembled to every breath of wind and made it seem cooler than it really was; somewhere toward the Avon a fox barked, and nearer—much nearer—a pair of hedgehogs snuffled out their courtship. I wondered whether, if they bit my ankles, I should know about it. When I was about four years old, a kitten slithered off my lap and left claw marks on my leg which turned septic because no one knew about them. There was an awful fuss. The nurses seemed to think it was my fault. I smiled deliberately into the darkness and listened to the traffic on the motorway. It came and went rhythmically as it crossed the bridge. A bit like

Number One in the pop charts of a month ago. I wondered what was Number One now. There was so much to catch up, so much to do. I must think about Mrs. Tirrell. And try to find out how Casey was progressing with Beamish.

And then, somewhere behind Mr. Ottwell's massed flowers, gravel crunched beneath a set of wheels.

I was so relieved I slumped in my chair, lowering my head and closing my eyes while my nerves trembled into quiescence. It had seemed like an hour waiting there. And with each minute that passed I had felt I'd burned my own boats. If Hawkins did not come he must have accepted my ultimatum. That would be . . . that.

When I raised my head he was just getting onto the big lawn. I heard him grunt as his wheels stuck in the dewy turf, and I remembered that his arms wouldn't be as comparatively strong as mine. Also that his stumps were aching to glory. I pushed myself forward furiously to meet him.

His face was a white blur against the darkness of the hedge. I got the impression of fair hair curling down quite long, a big head, a cricketer's head rather than a soccer player's, bony hunched shoulders, very long arms.

He gasped, "Christ, everyone will see you! Why the hell are we meeting *here*?"

Of course he'd observed me before and had no need for the questing, curious pause.

I said, "Because we both know it. Never mind now. Turn back onto the path and we'll go down the laurel walk." That meant I wouldn't be able to examine him much—it was very dark between the thick laurels—but I had already seen why he couldn't accept himself as a human being anymore. The rug which had swathed him securely in the art room that night had been replaced by a thinner honeycomb blanket that made a plateau of his lap and then abruptly descended to the step of his wheelchair. He was so obviously truncated, at least a third of him gone. As he struggled ahead of me to mount the slight camber of the path, I looked at the dark outline of the third that rose from his chair. He had been tall and strong and the world had been at his feet. And now he had no feet.

I said, "Hawkins . . . thanks for coming."

He didn't speak as he slewed his chair to face down the path. Then I felt him turn toward me and for a long moment we faced each other, black silhouettes in the sooty shadow of the laurel. The sharp smell of the pungent leaves almost overrode his disinfec-tant-and-bandage aura.

I whispered timidly, "I know how you feel. But it *will* make you sleep. For one thing the smell is so marvelous."

Another silence and I was terrified he was gritting his teeth against pain, waiting for strength to get back to the house.

Then he gathered himself together. "Don't you dare go soft on me, Fanny Adams!" he hissed.

"There's no need to be insulting!" I came back, quick as a flash, my heart lifting again to the excitement of the night and the strange sounds and the wonderful freedom. "I just don't want you backing down now. This is only a preliminary. What I really want to do more than anything is—get outside in a thunderstorm."

"Oh God," he said, grimly resigned.

I went ahead of him and bent to the business of moving. I knew at the end of the laurel walk there was a path around the edge of the reedy lake I could see from my dormer, and the water would reflect the starlight. I wanted to see him.

He wasn't far behind—his arms were stronger than I'd thought—and I deliberately kept my back to him until we were on the edge of the expanse of water. Then I did one of my on-the-spot turns.

He just missed me. "Clever," he panted. "Very clever. What would have happened if I'd gone into the water?"

"I'd have pulled you out, of course. Have you brought the script?"

That gave him something to do while I looked at him. He started fishing about inside his sweater, muttering something about bossy females, and I watched him carefully.

There were signs of neglect. He had held out against a haircut but someone—not Casey—had shaved him and nicked his chin and neck in several places. Unless he had acne. He was thin too; his bones stuck out at his wrists, and his shoulders were sharp beneath his sweater; his fingers looked skeletal. He had a full mouth, relaxed and sullen now as he searched for the separate pieces of paper. His brows

132

were heavy and shadowed his eyes, giving another impression of withdrawal. No wonder Bennie had flapped that first night. Then he looked up and I saw his eyes were blue.

"What are you staring at?" he said, tightly and immediately angry.

"You."

He stared back. Then with a gesture of finality handed the script over to me.

"Listen Fanny. It's no good, is it? We're great on the phone. We help each other along—I can never thank you enough. But . . . well, we've said it all, haven't we?"

"That's why I want to look. So shut up, can you?"

"You *know*. I've told you. They end *there*. Okay?" He pushed the honeycomb blanket under his stumps.

I wrinkled my nose disdainfully. "I swim with Stella and Penny. You can't shock me. I want to look at you, not your accident." I waved my hand airily. "Take no notice of me. You had your turn when I didn't know you were around. Look at the lake and listen. There was a fox just now. Soak it up, boyo. It's all part of the treatment."

He snorted again, not a laugh. His teeth showed in a ghastly grimace. They were good teeth, even and white. A long nose and jutting chin.

He said, "Oh *Fanny* . . ." His neck was strong and full of funny knotty cords. He was much too pale. Even in this light I could see that. I'd been indoors for three weeks but I still had some tan from that hot June. He repeated, more loudly, "Fanny. I cannot

133

just sit here while you stare. I can't do it. I'll have to go."

"It's okay, I've finished. And you'd better hurry up and get outside pretty soon, else you're going to look like a slug."

"A slug?"

"One of those white ones that get under stones. Nasty."

"Thanks. Thanks a lot."

I put the script carefully into my tidy bag. Then I aligned my chair with his, sat up very straight and assumed the voice of a tour guide.

"Over there we have the Avon bridge carrying the M5 motorway into Somerset and Devon. Before that it stops at Clevedon, where live the Parrishes in a nice house overlooking the sea. You should go there."

"What? And have Aunt Nell fuss-assing me worse than my own mother! Who at least permits embarrassment to drive her into another room now and then."

"Certainly Aunt Nell would never go into another room. Unless it was to get a meal. But surely you find when you're with her the boot is on the other foot?"

"How d'you mean?" He didn't sound interested.

"Well, you're the one who is embarrassed. Having to watch her suffer."

He gave it a second's thought, then said impatiently, "Either way it's too tough. And not worthwhile."

"Oh it's worthwhile."

"We'll have to disagree there."

I said cheerfully, "Okay." I was tired to death. It

was like pushing a stone up a hillside. I took a very deep breath and dived in at the deep end. "When are you going to get up? Go to physio and have a go on the parallel bars? Try some crutches? Get fitted for your tin legs?"

He sighed. "Now we come to it. The object of the exercise. The pep talk. Christ, Fanny. I thought you might be a little less obvious. You're losing your touch."

"I want to know. So I asked. Are you going to tell me?"

"No. Because you already know. You're probably the one person who has no need to ask such stupid questions."

"Sorry Hawkins. I've obviously missed out somewhere. I don't know the answer. Naturally I am assuming that having walked you would like to walk again. I'm not in a position to judge, of course, never having walked at all."

He breathed heavily. "You bitch," he said.

I turned my chair without haste and began to move away. "Time we were going in. Take deep breaths and think quiet thoughts."

He tried to catch me up. "Look here, Fanny, I'm sorry I was reduced to name-calling. But you know bloody well you're being unfair."

I kept going slowly along the dark tunnel of laurel. The smell was overpowering. I said softly, "When, Hawkins? When are you going to start learning to walk again?"

He couldn't pass me. He could have stopped but

135

maybe he felt, as I did, that once he stopped he'd never start again.

"Go to hell," he suggested tersely.

I shut up until we were on the terrace. The window was still open, no one was about. We'd done it. We were back and undetected. I stopped and looked around at him. We were both having difficulty with our breathing. He stared back and suddenly the moon came up from behind the house and illumined his face. It was beautiful. He looked at me with his blue eyes and smiled unwillingly.

"We made it. Without anyone knowing—"

"That's just a taste of freedom, Hawkins." I was missing the phone. I wanted to say something and make a quick getaway. I maneuvered my chair into position for a straight run through the window and across the lounge. He would have to stop and close up. I'd be up the ramp and in the lift before he knew it. I controlled my breathing with an effort of will. "Just a taste of freedom. Think how it will be when you can get out of that chair and walk again."

He threw himself back in exasperation. "Fanny, stop it. Please. You know I don't want to stump around—always in pain—half a mile behind anyone else—."

"But you've *got* to, Hawkins! You *must* walk again!"

"Why? Can you give me one good reason why I should put myself through all that?"

"Of course I can." I put my hands on my wheels and got ready. "How the hell can you carry me over the threshold if you can't walk?"

I pushed hard and shot through onto the oak boards

of the lounge. There was complete silence except for the soft brush of my wheels. I was out in the corridor taking a run at the ramp when I thought I heard something. I backed into the lift, put my hand on the button to close the doors and then paused. But there was nothing. No laughter. No whispered recall. My outrageous remark lay somewhere on the terrace. Ridiculous. Foolish. And quite rightly discarded.

12

 THE SCRIPT WAS good. Really good. He'd made a scale diagram of the pool and positioned us and the audience, scribbled an outline, written in the dialogue with alternatives and still left us room for our own bits and pieces of ad-libbing. I couldn't imagine how he'd done it all in a single day. No wonder he'd been tired.

I had to go down to therapy if I wanted to be allowed in the pool, so there was no chance to phone him until just before lunch. The prospect of doing so was there from the moment I woke from a troubled sleep and reread the script. I wanted to get in touch with him again more than anything, yet I dreaded it. What would his attitude be? Had I gone too far last night with that pert and stupid remark? It assumed a hell of a lot—or did it? Surely in our circumstances it was obvious—all too obvious—that it meant nothing at all?

Casey noticed how much I'd sweated in the night and tried to veto the pool, but I wasn't having any. It wasn't so warm, so I got her to find the black cotton T-shirt with the long sleeves that did such a lot for my shoulders and arms, and insisted on going down for breakfast.

She said brusquely, "I'll wheel you. You need to save your arms for swimming."

She offered the excuse so I wouldn't faint with surprise at her suggestion of extra help. I grinned at her. "Okay. Thanks. But don't worry about me, Casey. I've been dreaming. I always sweat when I dream."

She sat the laundry basket on my lap and wheeled me into the lift.

"You don't have to rush at everything, Fran," she said conversationally as we went down. "You've got time for all your schemes. Take it easy."

I swallowed at how much she didn't know.

"I really do love you, Casey. And Beamish."

She gave me her most enameled glare. "I didn't mean that particular scheme, Fran. I can look after my own interests, thank you very much."

"I wasn't thinking of that." I swallowed again and grabbed at my cool. "But remember who was responsible for bringing you two together, won't you?"

The lift doors opened, and she snatched up the laundry basket and went ahead of me without any more suggestions about helping. I sat still until she rounded the corner to the laundry room and couldn't resist glancing over her shoulder at me. I winked broadly. Her mouth tightened against a smile.

Miss Hamlin said nothing about any increase in my "sensation area." I couldn't feel her fingers as they probed and massaged, but I knew she was doing her stuff because I could hear her breathing. I didn't say anything either. Maybe we'd both been wrong in the first place.

Anyway then I went back upstairs and stuck some more flowers on Zeek and saw to my many vases and put fresh lavender in my drawers and talked to Dorothy. And if I didn't phone Hawkins now it would be lunchtime and the play practice and no chance.

I dialed five. It burped half of once.

"I just wanted to say—thanks a million for the work you did on this script. It's terrific. It really is great. Honestly."

Did he sound—yes he did—awkward. Embarrassed.

"It was something to do. A load of rubbish really. You don't have to use it you know."

"I know. But we will. We can really get cracking now. There's a practice after lunch." I didn't say, "How about coming?" or "We need our writer-in-residence" or anything like that. But the unsaid suggestion was implicit anyway.

He said, "Jolly good. Well . . . the best of luck with it. If you need any extra material . . . I mean, I timed it as best I could to about half an hour, but—"

"That's fine. Just fine. Honestly." This was terrible.

I ought to have snapped at him, "What's up, don't you want to marry me or something?" But I couldn't. If it hadn't been funny last night it certainly wasn't funny today. I said, "Oh excuse me, here's Casey. Good-bye." And put the phone down.

It was silent for about ten seconds, then it burped. About a quarter of once slipped by before I snatched it up. Here it was. He was going to say, "Listen, about your suggestion last night, I planned to live in sin if that's all right with you," and I would then say, "Sure, I planned that myself, so long as the bloke concerned has got a pair of legs." And it would be all right again. The fencing, the smart facade that kept any real meanings under wraps.

He cleared his throat, taken off guard by my quick reaction to that fraction of a burp.

"Oh . . . Fanny. I thought I'd just say—in case you didn't realize—*you* did the script. Okay?"

My heart dropped into the area where my big toe must be. I caught at my reserves and said, "Don't be idiotic, Hawkins. That's carrying modesty too far. Naturally I'm going to tell them who wrote it."

"No. I don't want them to know. It's important to me, Fanny—keep it to yourself, huh?"

Another special secret between us. He might still want to stay in his hole, but at least I was partially there with him.

"All right. But I feel rotten. Taking the credit for all your hard work. It's not fair."

"Life isn't. Haven't you noticed?" He made some awful noise to cover that remark and then said, "I

141

slept like a top last night. Thanks." And the phone went dead.

I spent a long time sifting that remark. It got me nowhere except to a decision that the next contact must be made by him. Right until twelve thirty that night I thought he'd ring and arrange to meet me by the lake. But he didn't.

Meanwhile the practice was a shambles. Naturally I suppose. We should have simply gone over the script and discussed it and sorted it out, but the kids were anxious to get in the water and we did nothing but shout our heads off at each other and yell, "Shut up!"

Before dinner we met up again and talked it over properly and Mrs. Tirrell took charge of the costumes, Henry the props, Granny and Mr. Pope the percussion instruments. Mrs. Pountney was still worried to death about tipping the chairs near the edge of the pool. It was a perfect excuse for ringing Hawkins and asking his advice. But I didn't.

For the next couple of weeks I was schizophrenic. Half of me was busy and excited and full of ideas for the show; the other half just waited, getting deader and deader as each day went by and the phone didn't ring. The excited half then got more excited to stop the dead half asking such questions as: Why when it seemed so real and special to me didn't it seem real and special to him? Hundreds of questions like that. And the only answer was that I was wrong. My senses were wrong; my special feeling about people was wrong; and my special, special feeling of exhilarated

142

anticipation was wrong. Wrong. Wrong.

It was strange though. During those two weeks I became very popular at Thornton Hall. If I'd wanted power then, I had it for that time. It seemed everyone deferred to me, asked my advice, laughed when they saw me coming. Aunt Nell and I grew into close friends; naturally she did not realize she was friendly with only half of me and she took to coming along to every rehearsal, even to donning a ghastly bathing suit to join us in the pool. Discussing the show with Uncle Roger one Sunday, she posed the problem of the chair tipping.

"Mrs. Pountney is very worried, dear—and I'm not surprised. Mrs. Gorman and Mr. Pope are not really up to judging the correct positioning of the chairs. And they are exceedingly stubborn about allowing the girls to help them."

"It's just that we wanted it to be *our* show," I explained. "We don't mind them being around—in the background—but when they have to crouch in front of the chairs and shout at Gran and Pope like talking direction finders it's a bit off."

Uncle Roger suggested we take a walk to the pool and have a look at the possibilities. I showed him Hawkins' plan—my plan as everyone thought—and he hummed and haaed and walked along the edge of the pool and eventually said it was impossible.

"But we're *doing* it," I bleated. "Okay we're doing it with the helpers, but we're doing it."

"With great care and no spontaneity by the sound of things," he said.

143

"Well . . ."

He knelt on the bank and laid his arm along the concrete edge.

"Listen Fran, how about this: a rubber buffer just here—say about eight feet long. And there—and nowhere else—is your ducking entry. If I can find some way of anchoring it—it'll have to be very strong—Granny and old Pope can be either side of the chair in full view of the audience. The girls can be behind providing the pushing power. They shove the chair hard against the buffer and the occupant will shoot out anyway. You can disguise the buffer as rocks—or hedge—or whatever."

"Hey. That's great!"

Aunt Nell smiled and smiled. "Uncle Roger is an engineer, you know, Frances dear. He has his own factory. When he gets an idea—"

"I'll have to ask permission to chop up the concrete a bit," he mused. "But if I promise to put it back as I found it, that shouldn't be too difficult. How long have I got Fran?"

"Till next Saturday."

He made an appalled face but he'd known he had only five days anyway. He simply wanted Aunt Nell and me to be full of admiration for his energy and efficiency and imagination. We were.

That night again I waited until one thirty before switching off my light. I knew by five past midnight that it was hopeless but I waited anyway. Zeek had flowers inside as well as out now, and he guarded the doorway impassively. The moths beat on my dormer. Dorothy sprawled, the wound in her stomach showing all too clearly my botched stitches. I tried to tell myself it was all the same, gloriously isolated and secure. But it was more than that now. It was also lonely. And a small wind blew through me though the room was draft proof.

Saturday came at last. The weather was just right; sunny with a bit of a breeze to cool down flushed faces and a few very high white clouds holding no rain. We hoped. The visitors started arriving at two o'clock, and at half past two the Fete was opened by an actor from the Bristol Old Vic. We showed them around meticulously. Our rooms, the library, the lounge and dining room and games room, the chapel which was a copy of a church in Constantinople, the O.T. rooms laid out with our work; the room where the kids had their school—and their stuff was really something—the physiotherapy hall with its ropes and machines; the grounds. There were cream teas on the terrace, and the band from the local Boys' Brigade played raucously and marched on the lawn. There were stalls and lottos and raffles and pinning the tail on the donkey. And all the time we eyed each other as we passed; our excitement only just contained within our social skins. No one was allowed to see the pool. We had told the helpers what we wanted, and they were busy within the stifling plastic cover doing their best for us. At half past four we went to change.

Aunt Nell had made me a lovely fishtail. I'd practiced in it a couple of times, and it gave no extra resistance to the water and kept my legs together too, so that swimming was easier than usual. It was made of that glittery Lycra stuff, and when I pulled myself up on the raft, the water ran off it in glistening drops. Casey helped me to pull it on and fasten it around my waist and under the fringe of green raffia seaweed that draped my shoulders. I hadn't had my hair cut since before I came to Thornton Hall and it was below the nape of my neck, but not long enough to do much draping. I'd vetoed a wig. The raffia had been Mrs. Tirrell's compromise.

She looked marvelous in a dress with an enormous skirt full of pockets, each one containing a doll that she would produce and throw into the water as she wailed, "I don't know what to do . . . o . . . o." Dennis was in tights and a black jacket and cocked hat with a plastic sword by his side. Rosie of course had a red hooded cape, which she could discard easily in the water. Penny and Stella wore identical smocks made of cheesecloth and ridiculous little hats with enormous bows, and Henry had a stuffed parrot on his shoulder as Long John Silver. Granny and Mr. Pope hardly needed to dress up as Malice and Mischief.

We covered ourselves in our black and white sheeting, took our instruments and lined up in position before the audience arrived. Bennie fluttered in the background by the tape recorder. Our end of the pool had been hung with curtains to represent a cave. There were plastic flowers and shells and fishnets everywhere. The yellow light filtering through the cover and hitting the water reflected back on us weirdly. We sat very still, petrified with sudden stage fright as Bennie started playing *Fingal's Cave* and the doors at the end opened to let in our audience. It was dreadful. We were like butterflies pinned in position. We couldn't move. Tentatively Mrs. Tirrell touched her triangle and Henry tried a roll on the drums as the sea music rushed in. The rest of us were glued to our chairs, unable to move a muscle.

And then Aunt Nell slipped sideways through the door, looked for me and waved. Someone spoke to her; she pointed and I could see her lips saying, "Yes. My niece. She's mostly responsible for the production." And the pride in her face was unmistakable. Well, you can't let someone like Aunt Nell down, so I started shaking my tambourine, and that was the signal for Granny to let fly. She hadn't forgotten a thing since her Salvation Army days. Before the audience had found their seats they were applauding her. She sat there, grinning toothlessly—she said she couldn't concentrate on keeping her teeth in when she played the tambourine—and she put that tambourine through its paces, ribbons flying, clappers clapping and *Fingal's Cave* completely ignored in the background. Dear Bennie changed the tape hastily for a Sousa march and Granny elbowed me fiercely and went into a quick tempo.

We were all going like the clappers when I realized Aunt Nell had disappeared again. Everyone had found seats. Beamish was in the front grinning like crazy; Miss Hamlin stood at the side tapping her foot to the music. There was no Aunt Nell; no Uncle Roger. Three empty seats right at the back next to the door; the roof about to blow off with rhythm and excitement

147

and no Aunt . . . thank God, here they came. Uncle Roger first, then Aunt Nell hovering nervously. And then . . . and then . . . someone else. Someone on crutches, one trouser leg pinned, a single artificial leg stumping, pushing, heaving, until the body could lurch forward onto the crutches again. Forward, struggle, upright . . . forward, struggle, upright. Three whole steps and then he waited and looked for me.

I could see his face clearly now. It wasn't so white and I fancied it wasn't so thin. His hair was golden blond and very curly. His shoulders squarer than ever because of the upthrusting crutches. I just stared at him. He was wearing gray flannels and a white shirt and a tweedy jacket. And he was saying—I could hear him inside my head—"This is what I've been doing for the past fortnight. This is why I didn't ring you. I wanted to show you instead."

I put my tambourine on my lap and lifted my hand and above the strident enthusiasm of Sousa I mouthed one word. "Thanks."

How could the show be a flop after that? It had to be a success with our writer sitting there watching his creation come to life. We went through all the business about rehearsing for a musical concert we didn't want to do. We announced our wished-for roles without embarrassment and with a lot of ham acting that started the laughter before we'd expected it. Granny cackled out the word "Malice" until it positively hissed over the water; Mr. Pope produced his single "Mischief" in a falsetto voice with eyelashes fluttering. At Granny. But the audience loved it. Mrs.

Tirrell suddenly announced she "had so many children she didn't know what to do" with a hard glance at someone on the other side of the pool, so that mentally I rocked back on my heels at the realization of her implacable anger for her husband. Dennis piped out "Captain Hook," then cleared his throat and repeated it in a growl. Stella and Penny spoke in absolute unison with identical lisps. Henry shuffled and was self-conscious. I was just   so happy.

Then came our acting bits. Stella and Penny first because they could bolster each other up. They had expanded a ditty Hawkins had written for them. It began "Two little maids from school are we, Sitting forlornly beneath this tree"—they erected a coverless umbrella hung with paper leaves amid a roar of appreciation. "No cake, not even a cup of tea; No hope of rescue for her—or me—" they went on, large eyed, their poor hands hidden beneath the masking sheets. We all began to relax. By the time they flung off their covering and ducked their heads to pull on their hats, no one noticed they were armless. Surely Hawkins would see that?

Granny came to the edge of the pool and bawled confidentially, "They'll never be the Babes in the Wood. But I can be Malice. And *he* can be Mischief." And she and Pope took a handle each, drew back the wheelchairs and shoved hard against our rubber buffer. Penny and Stella took off beautifully, curled themselves into balls and plopped into the water amidst gasps of shock and then thunderous applause. They came up and paddled around the perimeter like little ducks, trailing their cheesecloth plumage behind them. Miraculously their hats stayed in place. They were soon joined by Dennis, brandishing his sword and slicing magnificently at the water; Rosie, more gently lowered in by some of the helpers to float like an autumn leaf, her head pillowed on a foam float; Mrs. Tirrell swimming after her dolls, and Henry making awful parrot noises. And lastly, me.

The idea was that I should bring peace from confusion, and this was a bit of an anticlimax with the audience clapping and stamping all the time and the atmosphere in the pool riotously enjoyable. But I wasn't playing to them, I was playing to Hawkins. As soon as I surfaced, the strains of "The Beautiful Blue Danube" sifted through the medley of other noises and took my hands with it. I lay on my back and let them move on their own—this was something I hadn't been able to rehearse—and gradually everything quietened down and went very still so that my fingers and wrists and arms were the only moving objects. As if drawn by them I made for the float, pulled myself up and continued with the dance, and at a signal from Bennie the others began to glide toward me. We ended with a tableau; Malice and Mischief cowered in their chairs behind us.

The applause was deafening and went on and on until we didn't know what to do with ourselves. At last Beamish stood up and lifted his hands. "Ladies and gentlemen . . ." He made a little speech telling them about our rehearsals and our independence and thanking "our good friends the Parrishes" for their help. Then he said we would continue to swim for

150

a while and if anyone wished they could stay behind, but he would remind them that our evening meal was served at . . . I kept my eyes on Hawkins. When he stood up with help from Uncle Roger one side and Aunt Nell the other—how he must *hate* that—I wanted to applaud *him*. It wasn't fair that no one had recognized his part in the proceedings. They weren't even noticing what he was doing right at this minute. He didn't look at me again. As he started the rhythmic swing, push, stand . . . swing, push, stand, all over again, Aunt Nell turned and waved and then blew me a kiss. On an impulse I blew her one back.

He rang at eleven thirty.

"How about a turn around the garden before bed?" he said casually.

"Umm . . . well. All right. I suppose my knitting can wait till the morning."

"Oh I should think so," he said.

He was already by the window in the lounge and held it open for me. He was in his chair. We didn't say much, actually, and when we did we didn't fence anymore. I remember there was a bird. "Nightingales," he identified. "They like this weather. And the avenue." I realized the breeze of the afternoon had gone and the stillness no longer had a waiting about it. It was peace.

"You know about birds?" I asked.

He didn't make any funnies, just said, "A little. It's something I'll be able to follow up now."

I remember the heady scent of the stocks. And telling him what each flower bed contained in the

151

inky blackness of the sheltering hedges.

"Some of the staff call you the flower girl," he said with a smile in his voice.

"I'm very interested in flowers. Maybe next year I'll try for a Botany O level." I knew I wouldn't, but it was a small offering in exchange for what he had done for me.

I remember the myriad small sounds by the marshy lake and the way the water carried the noise of the motorway traffic as it pounded down to the West for holidays, or pounded back.

We returned very slowly between the acrid laurels.

"The Parrishes say their car will take two wheel-chairs," he mentioned hesitantly. "Could we visit them together?"

"Yes." A small spurt of excitement pierced the peace of my soul. "If only it would rain again. We might persuade them to let us go out in it."

He didn't laugh. "Not likely. You might get pneumonia again."

"Me? Don't be daft. That was a leftover from hospital. After nearly two months at Thornton Hall I'm as strong as an ox."

Why did I have to say that? To boast? To mislead him?

He didn't argue, just ran his chair up the ramp and along the terrace. I waited for him in the lounge to close the window and we exchanged silent smiles in the white moonlight. Then he went along the corridor to room five. And I took the lift to room seventy-eight.

13

 GRANNY SURVEYED us both with chin unusually well tucked in.

"What do you mean, it's a pity it didn't rain? You've had a day by the seaside, got yourselves nice and brown, and you wanted it to rain? Didn't you enjoy it?"

Mr. Pope muttered as a sort of background to this, "Ungrateful, that's what the young people are today. Ungrateful."

Hawkins said seriously, "I quite agree, Mr Pope. One wonders what will happen to the world if such ingratitude continues to—"

"I *told* you, Granny! We can usually persuade Aunt Nell to agree to things, and it's our only chance—"

Dennis pushed his chair backward and forward,

coming nearer to Mr. Pope's toes each time. "They want to go out in the rain," he explained impatiently. "Well, Fran does. And I do too. I want to drink the rain."

"Unhygienic," Hawkins mentioned. "Probably unhealthy too."

"Mad," chipped in Mr. Pope.

"I don't understand it." Granny was reluctant to agree with Pope.

"Reveals an unexpectedly shallow mind," Hawkins prosed on, avoiding my eyes lest he burst out laughing. "Which is understandable in the case of young Makepeace perhaps—" Young Makepeace tried to hit him and failed. I shoved him instead.

"Look." I went back to Granny and Pope. "What paraplegics want more than anything is . . . sensation. Surely you can understand that? We're missing out with half our bodies. So the other half demands more. Much more. We need a lot of time to look and smell and *feel.*"

It didn't seem to make much impression on the oldies and Dennis didn't get what I was talking about, but Hawkins stopped mucking about and looked interested.

"That's why you're always so busy, of course." His eyes looked gray today and I wondered whether yesterday's trip to Clevedon had tired him. "And why you're so . . . so wound up."

"Well"—Granny was tart—"it'll probably rain when we have our trip to Weston. So you two will be pleased even if it's ruined for the rest of us."

154

Mr. Pope howled as Dennis ran a wheel against his foot.

"Blasted kids!" he yelped.

Hawkins said solemnly, "I couldn't agree more, Mr. Pope."

It had been marvelous at Clevedon. We'd gone on Sunday morning and listened to the church bells and watched the promenaders taking dogs and children for an airing. The tide had been out, revealing an ugly muddy nudity that we had found vulnerable and appealing. We ran our chairs down the ramp and onto the slipway, to Aunt Nell's horror.

"What would have happened if you'd gone off the edge?" she asked later, still a bit trembly as she served lunch.

"We'd have hit the rocks and the headlines," Hawkins told her.

She said, "Oh Luke . . ."

It was two weeks since our Fete Day and he was fully "integrated" into our peculiar society. Occasionally there would be times when he was silent and morose; not often. When he'd had a lousy session in physio and couldn't manage his new legs, then was the worst. He still refused to see his family; he said he wanted to be able to stand without crutches for their first visit.

In the afternoon Uncle Roger and Aunt Nell pushed us along cliff footpaths up a hilly headland where there was an old church and a graveyard full of leaning headstones. We rested and looked at the gray sea

155

and the gulls wheeling and screaming around a cluster of rocks. Aunt Nell and Uncle Roger sat down so that they were on a level with us. They smiled and fought for breath. Hawkins talked about the gulls and some ducks he'd seen on the way up. It seemed they should be nearer fresh water.

I said, "I like it here. I'd like to be put here when I die."

Aunt Nell reached for a laugh and Uncle Roger panted, "Fine. I'll keep a place next to me."

Hawkins didn't say a word. He flashed me a look which I couldn't identify, then his eyes seemed to go cold and opaque. Later, as we coasted back down the hill ahead of the mere pedestrians, he said tensely, "Don't ever say things like that again, Fanny. It's not funny."

"What isn't?" I knew. His prolonged silence had told me. He didn't bother to enlighten me. I blustered, "We all have to go, you know, Hawkins."

"Not for ages. And it's not funny."

He sounded so mad that I didn't mention the fact that I hadn't been joking or trying to create an effect. We reached the bottom of the hill and ran our chairs onto brittle grass, turned and waited for the others.

I said, "I'm sorry. Won't happen again."

He didn't even accept my apology, and I felt a little quiver of premonition. Suddenly he said, "I wish Roger would hold Nell's hand or something."

I glanced up as they came down the cliff path single file.

"It's not that steep."

"No. I just wish—sometimes—he'd . . . hold her hand."

I thought he was changing the subject and that my premonition had been a mistake. I thought he was a little embarrassed by his own intensity and his remark was a way of keeping his distance. And that was okay, wasn't it? We acted as stimuli on each other and that was enough. Somehow I would needle him into walking again and then he'd go home and I wouldn't see him again. And I didn't look properly at Uncle Roger and Aunt Nell.

The outing to Weston dawned breezy but cloudless. We went in two coaches with limited seating and plenty of space for our own chairs.

Mr. Pope said, "It'll be blowing half a gale along that seafront. You'll see."

Casey tucked a rug over his knees and checked he had his indigestion pills. "The forecast is that the wind will drop, Mr. Pope. I don't really think you need your winter overcoat."

He held on to it grimly, as if he expected her to rip it from his back. "Oh yes I do. It's always windy at Weston. Even when it's sultry everywhere else."

"Blow the cobwebs away then, won't it?" Granny cackled at him with her Jap officer teeth and opened her bag for me to see a stock of chocolate already disintegrating under pressure. I laughed—I hadn't done anything but laugh since I got up—and she cackled again and dug old Pope in the ribs. I waved through the window at Hawkins, Dennis and Rosie in the other coach. Mrs. Tirrell hovered about uncertainly between the two vehicles, waiting to see in which one Beamish would travel. It struck me then that maybe it wasn't simply coincidence that had separated Hawkins and me.

We got to Weston and Pope was right, it was blowing a force nine all along the fine-sand beaches. Our helpers had to pull us along in reverse to avoid silting us up completely; as it was you could taste the grittiness on your tongue and feel it beneath your eyelashes. We went early to the hotel where we'd booked luncheon, and they made a terrific fuss of us and took us into a gorgeous rest room on the ground floor where we could wash. Penny, Stella and I borrowed some of Casey's eye shadow and perfume and did ourselves up with her help. Then we went in to lunch like royalty and had drinks—proper alcoholic drinks—and canapés from a long side table and then took our places and were served by smiling waitresses. It was absolutely marvelous.

When the coffee came Beamish leaned over the table and said to everyone: "It's a bit tricky with this wind. Staff Nurse Casey has suggested the fun fair for our younger members. Perhaps an afternoon cinema would suit the rest of us?"

So we went to the fun fair.

Hardly anyone was there. It was right on the end of the Grand Pier and everything creaked and groaned in the wind and looked desolate. The fair people were delighted to see us. They lifted us in and out of the bumper cars, settled us securely on the wooden horses, strapped us into the figure-eight carriages.

Hawkins bowled up to the man in charge of the Ferris wheel.

"Can me and my girl have a ride? We've got thirty pence."

The rides were plainly marked twenty pence each, but the man beamed at us and stopped the wheel pronto. I hardly noticed being lifted in and clamped down with the safety bar. Hawkins had called me his girl.

At the top of the circle we could see right over Weston. There was the enormous bay fast filling with sea, the donkeys still battling gallantly along the sands, chip papers blowing along the prom. It was the most beautiful sight I've ever seen. I gasped and screamed little screams, and Hawkins put his arm along the back of the car and laughed with me. And then I lifted my face ecstatically.

"It's raining!" I called. "It's raining—" The sky was gray but cloudless and not a spot marked the scoured promenade.

"So it is!" yelled Hawkins without even a lifted eyebrow. He tightened his arm and pulled me close against him. "It's pouring. Pouring!"

We swept to ground level and had a quick vision of the man in charge gaping at us in amazement, then we climbed up again and left the mechanical racket far below us. The wind whipped my hair into Hawkins' face and he went on laughing through it. "We'll drown," I gasped into the wind.

"No we won't. I've got you. I'll hold you up."

159

There was confidence in his voice. More than confidence, a masculine boastfulness. It was the way a good-looking man, with legs and all his powers and strength, talks to a woman. A woman he wants to impress.

I looked around at him and stopped pumping out laughter. His eyes were striped gray and blue, his mobile mouth parted and grimaced against the gale. We stared. Then he kissed me.

"Fanny," he breathed against my lips. "Sweet Fanny Adams."

For once I said nothing. I was nothing. Only what Lucas Hawkins made me.

Beamish sat on the corner of his desk and looked at me with his round eyes.

"I'm speaking to you as a friend, Fran. Not as a doctor. As a friend."

"Okay. But you *are* a doctor."

"Roger Parrish would say the same thing to you."

"What about Aunt Nell?" His mouth twitched and I followed up quickly. "Don't be too sure. Aunt Nell knows me pretty well now. Which means she *trusts* me."

"So do I Fran. But you're only sixteen."

"And never been kissed," I quoted, my voice bitchy but my mood soaring in spite of everything. That kiss, that magic kiss on the Ferris wheel in the midst of our imaginary thunderstorm, had changed me. I had to preserve that changed Frances. No one, least of all Beamish, must spoil her. I decided to assume

160

that the subject was now closed and I said in my ordinary voice, "That reminds me. How are you making out with Casey these days?"

He took a breath, then let it out, capitulating.

"Fran. If you were a sixteen-year-old girl with legs that worked I would probably tell you to mind your own business at this precise moment." He smiled very slightly to take the sting out of his words. "So. Mind your own business."

I smiled too, well pleased with his reply. "If it *was* my business because I happened to think a great deal of the two parties concerned, I would still be very happy with that answer, Brother Beamish. It tells me a lot."

He gasped a laugh. "You're incorrigible!" He jabbed a long finger at me. "But you've given me my reason for telling you to go easy with Luke Hawkins. It's not because this is a residential home with rules and regulations. But because I think a great deal of the two parties concerned."

The subject wasn't closed. I didn't want to talk about it but he was going to make me. When he'd met me—very casually—as I came out of physio and asked me about my increase in sensation, I had known something else was on his mind. He'd walked along to his office as we talked, so that I had to follow. Then he'd suggested quietly that Luke and I were becoming "too exclusive." I'd simply laughed at first. It was such a crazy description of Luke and me. I couldn't take Beamish seriously. Even when he said, "I'm speaking to you as a friend," I was too euphoric to absorb what he was saying. Now I knew how serious he was. He was relating his feeling for Casey to Luke's for me. He was taking us very seriously indeed.

I blurted defensively, "You started it. You and Uncle Roger and Aunt Nell—weeks ago, before I was ill—you thought I might be able to use my feminine wiles to—"

He leaned forward suddenly and took my hands in both of his. I realized then that they had been fighting the air in protest. Sketching an invisible wall between us.

"Fran. Dear Fran."

He stilled me with that magic touch of his. His hands knew mine. Used to probing the human skeleton through its barrier of flesh and skin and nerve ends, his phalanges locked on mine and held me still, right through to my soul. He kept looking at me until all the defenses had gone. Then he spoke very quietly indeed.

"You love him, don't you?"

Tears flooded my eyes. I had tried so hard not to analyze what I felt for Luke Hawkins; simply to glory in it. Now I knew there was no need for analysis. I loved him. This was what love was. All the reading I had done was useless and stupid and completely misleading. Love play. The French kiss. Orgasms. Other things that could never be for me because I had no feeling below hip level. They were nothing. Nothing. Nothing. Because without them I could still love. With my mind and soul. And with my body. My pulsating, beating body.

Beamish whispered insidiously, "Then you already know, Fran. You know it cannot be. You know you cannot hurt him."

I swallowed my tears. "He loves me too!" It sounded like a cry for help in the sunlit dust-moted room.

"Does he? Is he as . . . committed . . . as you are, Fran? You're clever. Can't you turn it into something else?"

First, the implanted doubt: Did Hawkins love me *really*? Beamish and I knew what the *really* meant. It meant: Would Hawkins have looked twice at me if his legs were still there? Wasn't he intrigued and excited because I'd constantly needled him until I'd scalpeled my way under his skin?

It was Beamish who was the clever one. Maybe that doubt had been there all the time like a dormant cancer, but he'd brought it to life. It grew beyond a doubt into a fact in approximately two seconds.

Next he dished up a compliment. A double compliment really. I was clever. Not half so clever as Beamish of course, but clever. Clever enough to take control of Hawkins' feelings and divert them into safe channels. That was, of course, if they needed diverting. My God. My mind whirled between the doubt and the certainty. I felt sick.

I said very clearly, "You don't object to a flirtation?" My hands tried to move in his. "Just enough to get him going so that he'll keep trying with his tin legs? Maybe I should let him touch me up a bit? After all I couldn't feel a thing and if he could get through

163

my plastic pants and the sanipads it might give him an extra thrill. Wouldn't you say?"

His grip hurt like hell.

He said in a hard voice, "You know bloody well what I mean. Look at the alternatives, Fran—for Christ's sake. Do you go on as you are now until Luke's whole world is Fran Adamson and then say, 'Yes, we've got something special, but not for long because I forgot to mention that besides being paraplegic I've got a dicky heart'? Is that how you plan it, Fran?" I knew this was hurting him because he was the most unbrutal man in the world. He had to goad himself on. "What do you think that will do to Luke Hawkins?" The black eyes were chips of coal. "He might even hate you. You've only seen one side of him, Fran. He can be a pretty vicious human being. Ask Bennie. Ask Casey if you like. How do you think his parents feel not seeing him all these weeks?"

I twisted at my hands uselessly and avoided the main question. "He's trying to spare them the pain of seeing him helpless—"

"Rubbish!" he said curtly. "He's trying to hurt them, Fran. A lot of accident victims do it. They're shouting at the tops of their voices: Why should it be me and not you!" There was a long silence into which our breathing pumped jerkily. Then he said quietly, "Fran, you're stronger than he is. Believe me. At the moment you're giving him some of your strength. Because he believes you're in this together. But when he finds out—*if* he finds out—"

I couldn't free my hands, so I twisted my head away and whined like a little kid: "I don't see why we can't have a little time together. A year. Maybe two."

He said levelly, "Love makes people vulnerable, Fran. If you make Luke vulnerable, when he finds out he'll feel you cheated him and he might hate you. If he doesn't find out until"—even Beamish hesitated here—"until after, then he'll be hurt. Either way he's in for a lovely time."

I wanted to cry, but I fought to keep my anger in the belief that it would sustain me.

"So we're back to the flirtation. Just a gentle one, of course. So that this time next year he'll visit me now and then as a duty and forget me as a person." This was exactly how I'd worked it out when we were in Clevedon. I grabbed the arms of my chair and hung on tight. That had been before Weston. Before the Ferris wheel. Before Hawkins had kissed me and whispered, "Sweet Fanny Adams."

I choked on some bile. "You want me to sacrifice my *identity* for Luke Hawkins!" I looked up at Beamish balefully like an animal. "Next thing, you'll be saying that's the way to prove I really love him." I opened my mouth to say more and it stayed open on those last words.

He got off his desk and went to the door and held it open for me. He didn't say another word. I guess he thought I'd said it all.

I don't remember getting up to my room. Zeek and Dorothy watched me as I wept. I couldn't stop.

That evening when it was beginning to get dark—the nights were drawing earlier as August wore on—Casey knocked on Zeek and came in.

I said wearily, "Why are you here? You should have gone home ages ago."

"Douglas is taking me to the theater. So I stayed and had dinner here."

I saw she was dressed in something long and midnight blue. Her hair was around her shoulders.

"You look more like Marilyn Monroe than ever." It was the best I could do in compliments. "And why are you telling me you're going out with Beamish? It's not like you to be so forthcoming."

"Because I wouldn't be going out with him if it weren't for you, would I?" She began briskly to tidy up the things I had discarded during the long afternoon. Scissors I'd got out and not used, magazines and records, a long skirt I was shortening, my books about Dylan Thomas. "My turn for a question. Why did you miss tea and dinner today?"

"Tired."

"They sent something up for you and you returned it untouched."

"Unhungry."

"I see. Bennie says if you drop into the kitchen in half an hour you can have coffee and biscuits with her."

"She usually brings them up about tennish."

Casey straightened abruptly. "Oh she does, does she? That woman will never make a nurse!" She went to the door and put something on my dressing table as she passed. "Well. Luke Hawkins is waiting for you in the garden. So I thought if you had a chat with him you might feel like a hot drink afterward. On your way back to bed."

My eyes focused on her. She stood at the door all sapphire and gold, watching me.

"It's against the rules to go out after dinner," I croaked.

"I understand you do it often, however. The French window in the lounge is left undone for the dogs. And you never seem to disturb anyone."

"I can't see him. Not yet. And certainly not alone."

"He's waiting for you."

"Beamish says—"

"I know what Beamish says." Her voice was very level. Of course—they'd eaten dinner together and probably talked about me. "Sometimes—not often—Beamish talks through his hat." She smiled gloriously and pointed to the dressing table. "Borrow my perfume if you like. And if you're not back in the kitchen in half an hour, Bennie will be out to look for you. That gives you about fifteen minutes to talk to Luke Hawkins. Surely you can face him for that long?"

I tried to thank her, but Zeek was between us.

On the way down I planned it carefully. He was going to be anxious because I hadn't appeared all day and I was going to tell him I'd been ill and that I often was and he'd have to get used to it. I was going to have to let him kiss me again, else he'd suspect something, but after that we'd look at the flowers or listen to the nightingales, then I'd say I wasn't too good and had got to get in. I'd be dull. I'd be heavy and dull. Because of my weight I'd slip—gradually, very gradually—through his fingers.

That was the way to play it. That was the way I was going to play it. Until I saw him.

He was in full view of everyone on the open part of the horseshoe lawn. I bowled frantically toward him gesturing him to get in the shadow of the aspen. He went ahead of me, turned, opened his arms. Our chairs clashed together; we managed as best we could. He kissed me again and again, smoothing the hair back from my hot face, pushing away the tears with his fingers. The awful day began to recede. Maybe, after all, I'd encapsuled the magic out of Beamish's reach.

When at last I calmed down, he whispered, "What is it? Tell me, Fanny. What's happened? I've been frantic all day, and when you wouldn't answer the phone I came up in the lift and Beamish was waiting for me at the top and told me you had to rest—God, it was awful. What happened?"

I forgot my resolutions in panicked horror. "The phone didn't ring—they must have disconnected me!" For a blind moment I wanted to get out then and there. I fought to be fair to Beamish. "He was trying to give me some privacy. To sort myself out." I gulped and hung on to Hawkins' wide shoulders and changed my story on the spot. I don't know why. Except that I had to have Hawkins on my side. I had to. I gave him half the truth.

"He talked to me, Luke. Before lunch. I had extra physio and Miss Hamlin thinks I might be getting back some feeling and—and Beamish talked about that, then about us. We have to cool it, Luke."

I started crying all over again, and he gripped me hard so that my face was pushed into his neck and I

168

could feel all those cords and the power and strength of him. His legs were gone but his strength was still all there, concentrated into the other two thirds of his body. I wished he would crush me into him; I wanted to become part of him, breathe with his lungs, look through his eyes.

He spoke in a low voice, a growl of anger.

"We'll get out of here, Fanny. Tomorrow. I'll ring up my father and he'll take us both. You'll be eighteen soon and we can get married without anyone's permission—Christ, how *dare* he speak to you like that? As if we were freaks or something."

Now was the time. It was here now. Upon me. I must tell him the truth.

I moved my head and felt the roughness of his twelve-hour beard against my cheek.

"Don't be daft, Hawkins." I clamped down on those wretched tears. "We can't get *married*. Not like that. I'm not upset—honestly—not anymore. He has to make a bit of a protest—rules and regulations and so on—but he's marvelous really."

I would tell him in a minute, of course. But first I had to know if Hawkins had really asked me to marry him. He had, hadn't he? I mean no one had asked me before or was likely to in the future. I had to know.

He said, "Of course we can get married. That's what this is all about, Fanny, remember? I'm going to carry you over the threshold and—"

"I was joking," I said weakly.

"Well, I'm not." He held me up by my shoulders.

169

His eyes were black in the darkness. "We're going to get married, darling. That is definite. The one certain thing in our uncertain future. And if there's going to be a lot of fuss here about us making that obvious, then we will go. Leave." He darted a kiss at me and pulled back to stare again, trying to convince me with his seriousness. "Listen, Fanny Adams. Sweet, sweet Fanny Adams. My parents—my whole blasted family—are rich. You've heard of Hawkins' paper mills? That's us, baby. And money can do things. Oh, I know when I arrived here I thought I'd reached the limit of what it could do for me. But now . . ." He kissed me again. "My parents will adore you, Fanny. They'll see that it's you who have brought me back to life and they'll adore you. Dad will have ramps put everywhere and get you a car with hand controls—oh Fanny, let's go. Let's go tomorrow. Please."

I stared back at him while his words made pictures in my mind. A house. Everyone except Hawkins and me walking. And soon Hawkins would be walking too. Maybe getting a job at the paper mills and becoming independent. I had to *tell* him!

I whimpered, "I couldn't live in a house, Hawkins. I've always lived in hospitals and institutions."

"Then it's time you had a home. Your own home."

Oh, he knew me better than I knew myself. My own home.

I bleated, "It would be your parents' home, Luke! Not mine!"

"At first. Then we'd get our own place, Fanny. Smaller. Maybe at Clevedon, huh? Near Aunt Nell?

170

One of those little cottages where you could run down to the beach anytime you wanted."

My heart was twisting with agony.

I whispered, "I couldn't live away from medical help, Hawkins. I have drugs every day. And I wet myself. I smell."

He still held me at arms' length when I wanted to bury my burning face into his neck.

He said steadily, "Fanny. Do you love me?"

"Yes."

"Then why won't you trust me?"

I couldn't stop the tears then. He had no idea what he was asking when he said that. Oh God . . . why couldn't I trust him? Why couldn't I tell him the simple truth? Was it that, in spite of everything, I *still* put myself first? Was it because I couldn't bear it if Beamish was right and he turned from me in anger? Or even if he wasn't right and Hawkins stayed close to me—only differently—wearing kid gloves and treating me as if I were made of glass? No more midnight phone calls in case I was tired. No more swimming in case it overtaxed my heart and lungs. Yes, I put my own feelings first. A man—a strong, good-looking man—had asked me to marry him. I couldn't put aside that beautiful compliment. Not yet. Not just yet. I hated myself, but I went on crying and let him fold me to him and stroke my face and hold my earlobe and tell me everything would be all right.

We were still and quiet after a while. I lay on his chest with my eyes closed and promised fate that I would carry out my original plan quite soon. After

171

just a little while. A day or two. Or perhaps a week. I would be dull and heavy.

I lay there. He ran his hand across my forehead, tracing the outline of my nose, mouth and chin, down my neck, across my left shoulder and down the full length of my arm. He took my hand, squeezed it, came up the inside of my arm, across my breasts, down to my waist, right around my body and then I lost him over my hips.

He said, "You are the most beautiful creature I have ever seen."

I tingled with sensation from the waist up. I put my hand up and pressed against the back of his head and kissed him with open mouth.

He muttered, "You smell of flowers—my flower girl."

I breathed a laugh and recognized it for one of triumph.

"That's Casey's perfume," I said with down-to-earth honesty.

He pushed his face into my neck. "I still love your smell." He looked up as our chairs parted.

I said, "You don't know my smell. You've never smelled me. I'm all deodorant."

"And flowers." He caught my hand. "I *love* you."

I moved my arm into the moonlight to see my watch.

"We've got two minutes to get to the kitchen before Bennie sounds the alarm." I smiled at him blindly. "Hawkins. I hope Miss Hamlin is right."

"Huh?"

I shoved off and he had to follow.

172

"She says I might one day be able to feel below my hips."

He was silent till we reached the terrace. Then he said grimly, "We'll manage, Fanny. Whatever they say, we'll manage. Just trust me, my darling."

He went ahead of me to pull open the French door into the lounge, and I wondered what trust had to do with it. Facts were facts. Wet knickers were wet knickers and maybe that was what Hawkins had felt when his hands had gone below my "sensation area."

14

 FOR THE REST OF that week
Hawkins was solidly, defiantly, aggressively at my side.
He came with me to physio and made me wait while
he stumbled between the parallel bars on his alumi-
num legs. When Beamish was in sight he draped a
possessive arm across my shoulders. Most of his sentences began loudly with "When we're married . . ."

I begged him to shut up.

"Why?" He opened those blue-gray eyes of his until
they practically fell out. "Everyone's tickled pink. And
it's catching, too. Mrs. Tirrell's got tears in her eyes
every time she sees us. And as for Granny Gorman
and Mr. Pope, they're loving every vicarious moment."

It was true. And Stella and Penny couldn't leave

me alone. They were always knocking on Zeek to come in for girlish chats that could have been condensed into an awed "What's it *like?*"

I said, "Mrs. Tirrell's in an emotional mess. She adores Beamish—probably because he's unattainable—but if she goes all goo-goo over us she might murder Casey or something."

It was the nearest I could get to our previous flippancy. I was scared. I didn't know why. I was shit scared. Hawkins snorted a laugh; he was enjoying the situation—and that was part of the trouble. He'd phoned his parents and asked them over on Sunday to meet me. He felt wonderfully masterful. It made me remember my conversation with Miss Hamlin and how I'd felt that whatever was coming to me might be so tremendous it would be too much for me to handle. I shivered.

He said in a low voice, "Fan . . . what's the matter, love? You don't really mind people knowing, do you? I want to shout it from the roof. I'm so proud."

I shook my head. "I'm proud too. But it was our secret. Our special secret. . . . I don't know."

"You and your secrets. It's the little girl in you that must have secrets. In an institution the only safe way to keep anything to yourself is to make it secret. It's going to be different now, Fanny, because you're a big girl and because we're unbeatable when we're together. Won't you believe that?"

I nodded and reached for the reassurance of his hand. We were in the games room, alone. He pulled me forward in my chair and met me halfway. As he

175

kissed me I looked over his shoulder to see Beamish pushing at the swing doors. I squeezed my eyes tight shut and hung on to Hawkins as if I were drowning. When I surfaced, Beamish had gone.

They came on Sunday. Both tall and big; outdoor people. It was raining and they wore identical raincoats, khaki colored and voluminous and tatty in a frightfully posh way. They drew up chairs next to the billiard table—"We're booking it for later," chuckled Mr. Hawkins. "Though whether I can still beat Luke from this low level . . ." Luke said steadily, "Give yourself the same handicap as me, Dad. Play from a chair." Mrs. Hawkins flushed painfully and pressed back against the edge of the table. She was flat as a board and skinny in a sinewy tough way. She must have been well over thirty when she'd had Luke, and I got the feeling he might have been a mistake. Though her love for him now was agonizingly obvious, she didn't look the maternal type. The pregnancy was possibly an inconvenience coming in the middle of the tennis season and ending during the Ladies' Open Golf. . . . I cut off my thoughts and smiled gratefully at Aunt Nell, squatting close to my chair and looking as protective as a hen. Uncle Roger couldn't make it. He was on a business weekend. He'd offered no opinion on the subject of Hawkins and me. But Aunt Nell had. Somehow I'd known she would be on our side.

Luke went at it bullheaded.

"I've told you about Fanny—she likes to be called Fran by the way—she practically forced me to take part in the entertainment we did on Fete Day—"

"I do wish you'd let us come to that, old son. We'd have enjoyed seeing you get your accolade—"

"No one knew I'd done anything Dad. It was a secret. Anyway, then Fran and I started to meet—"

"Secretly?" asked Mrs. Hawkins, startled.

"Of course. And we went to Mrs. Parrish's house for the day and to Weston on our outing and gradually we came to realize that we were meant for each other. That's what the whole thing is about. . . ." He waved his hands in the air, exasperated with them for their questioning expressions. "I mean, why I pranged that bike! Why the paper mills make so much lucre! Why—why the universe *is*!"

Mr. Hawkins laughed a rumbly, comfortable, unflappable laugh. "I think our young man is in love, Marion," he said to his wife.

"Well done, Dad. Top marks."

Mrs. Hawkins tried hard to smile, but her facial muscles were set too rigidly. She said, "I can't quite . . . You met—face to face—at the Fete Day. Is that right?"

"Three weeks before then." Hawkins spoke with studied patience. "Then we kept away. I wanted to surprise Fanny by coming to the show on my legs. I couldn't have done it without Nell and Roger of course. I can still only manage about six steps, but—"

"And the Fete Day was July the twenty-sixth. Four weeks and a day ago. You've known each other four and a half weeks?"

"My God, Mother! We've always known each other!

177

We *recognized* each other! Can't you understand?"

"Hawkins . . . please . . ." I hung on to his arm. It was tensile and quivered within its steel hardness.

Aunt Nell lunged forward.

"Mrs. Hawkins—Mr. Hawkins—there's no explaining it. If you can wait—come and see them often—you will be reassured. And so happy for them."

"Of course," Mrs. Hawkins said, all uptight. "You have had the opportunity to be with them and see this—er—relationship develop."

"Yes, old son. It's hurtful to your mother and me that you have shut us out so completely. Until now. When apparently we are necessary."

Somehow Luke controlled himself. Aunt Nell stammered something placating while I felt through his arm how he forced himself to be calm and reasonable. About something that was assuredly neither calm nor reasonable.

He spread his hands, palms upward.

"Look Mum. Dad. I'm sorry. I behaved badly. But I thought you understood. I had to find my own way or die. And I admit I wanted to die. At least I thought I wanted—"

Thank God both the Hawkinses stumbled over their swift reassurance; Mrs. Hawkins got away from the table edge long enough to touch one of his hands.

He took in a breath. "And surely you're not of the school that thinks because I've lost my legs I should never get married and have kids and live normally?"

They went along with that too, shaking their heads emphatically and saying things that I didn't hear. Because I was stuck on what Hawkins had said. Kids. He planned on having kids.

Anyway it seemed everyone was in agreement after a stormy beginning. Aunt Nell was smiling and Mr. Hawkins was jovial and I let go the arm and sat back in case Hawkins should sense my shock.

He grinned at his father. "Well then, Dad. When can you come and fetch us? We'd better hang on until you've had a chance to get the rooms ready on the ground floor, I suppose. I've thought a lot about it. Fanny can have the room that looks over the river— from there she can get to the patio. If you could have a ramp fixed alongside the steps."

"Hang on, hang on, son. What's your hurry, for goodness' sake? Your Frances is sixteen as I understand it. You're eighteen. Even if you were both—" He broke off and stared at his wife.

Hawkins said, "Normal? If we were both normal, Dad?"

Mrs Hawkins pushed hard against the billiard table. "Darling—darlings—" She tried so hard to smile at me I could have wept for her. "Dad is right. There's no hurry. In fact just the opposite. You need the help they're giving you here, Luke. You said yourself you can manage only six steps on your artificial legs as yet."

"I can do exercises at home. Have a masseur around—"

"Then there's Fran. She needs medical care and attention surely?"

"Nothing that we can't provide for her at home,

179

Mother. Listen, I thought I explained this on the phone. They find it . . . inconvenient to have us here as we are. They're hot on mixing us all up—integrating us as they sickeningly put it. But when two of us fall in love and want to be alone and hold hands and kiss—"

Mrs. Hawkins withdrew and said on an indrawn breath, "Of course. Naturally. Surely you can see, Luke, that it isn't really the *thing*—"

Aunt Nell, who might well have used those identical words a few weeks ago, made another lunge. "There's nothing wrong about Fran and Luke's behavior, Mrs. Hawkins. They're so natural—"

Hawkins said impatiently, "Just take my word for it, Mother. It's becoming difficult here."

Mr. Hawkins rumbled into gear.

"I'm with your mother here, old son. Dammit all, life has to go on. Other people fall in love, you know. They have to go on working and looking after themselves and fitting in with other people."

"But we can't *do* that here, Dad. We need time and space to breathe in. We haven't got those things here."

"That's not true, Hawkins." It was the first time I'd spoken properly and everyone looked surprised. I cleared my throat and reached for Aunt Nell's hand. "It's not. Not strictly, you know. You're going off half cocked because Doc Beamish had a tactful word with me and I got upset. Which was silly of me. He hasn't said anything since. Not a word. He's accepted us . . . the situation."

Aunt Nell squeezed my hand. Hawkins said belligerently, "Then why open his big mouth in the first place?"

I said lightly, "I think one of the reasons might have just come up."

Hawkins frowned and looked like an irritable Norse warrior. "I don't get it."

"Well. I can't have children, Hawkins. I thought you'd realize that."

He went on frowning at me, then shook his head decisively. "I don't believe it. I told you the other night, we would manage. We *will*, Fanny. We will."

"I can't have kids, Hawkins."

Aunt Nell clung to me. We were two barren women together.

Hawkins rallied. "I don't care. D'you think I care about that? It's you I love. You. If you'd really believe *that*, Fanny, there'd be none of this arguing. Just believe it, will you?"

"I believe it. I'm just saying that's why Beamish put in the cautionary word."

"So. So he wanted to spare me. When there was no need. Because it doesn't alter the situation. We've got to get away and be together all the time without anyone interfering."

I smiled at his glorious selfishness. He was spoiled and self-willed and I loved him for it. I kept on smiling until his hard eyes softened. His parents were murmuring in the background about listening to Frances because she was talking such sense and her feet were so firmly on the ground. Feet! I ask you. But they meant well.

I said, "Like you keep mentioning, Hawkins, we'll

181

be okay. Here or anywhere. But no one will interfere with us here. Don't rush things—we're all right."

We were drowning in each other's gaze, as so often happened. I could feel my will swaying his. He turned away with difficulty.

"You know I want to marry Fanny as soon as possible?" he said to his parents.

His mother said, "I understand she is in the care of—"

"She'll be of age in another sixteen months," he interrupted impatiently. "Then no one can stop us."

"If you still feel as you do now, no one will try, old son," his father assured him. He smiled right at me and I suddenly realized his eyes were also stripy gray and blue. Maybe once he had loved Marion Hawkins as Hawkins now loved me. It was just possible.

In spite of it all ending amicably, there was a lot of arguing after they'd gone. Hawkins said he couldn't understand why I'd gone back on what we'd agreed all week. I said I hadn't agreed to anything whatsoever; I'd had a moment of panic, he'd reassured me and then acted as if the whole world were against us; there was absolutely no point in going to his parents' home immediately; let them get used to the idea he'd hurled at them. He said as I hadn't put up any objections he'd assumed I was with him all the way and he had felt completely let down that afternoon.

I said, "Balls."

He was sitting right in my dormer with the before-dinner light full on his curly head. He summoned a ghost of a smile at that.

"No. Honestly, Fanny. I felt you'd whipped the ground from under my wheels."

"You still managed to beat your father hollow when you played billiards."

"Oh, Fanny. Stop it. Talk properly to me."

"Okay. The ground was whipped away from you because I told you I couldn't have kids. I was like Aunt Nell. Barren. That's what has upset you."

"Balls to you!" He pushed his chair toward me and I retreated around the table. "Fanny." He stopped and pleaded at me and my heart melted. "Fanny. Fanny. Fanny. It's you I want. I want to stay with you all the time. I want to sleep with you. Now."

"Don't be daft, love."

"We've got to be frank about it, Fanny. Just because I haven't got any legs and yours don't work doesn't mean we can't have sex. There are people who will advise us about this. Okay, we'll have to work at it, but surely it will be worth it? Don't you want me like I want you?"

His eyes were dark with dilated pupils, his long mouth full and soft and pouting.

I said, "There's the dinner gong."

His pout became pronounced. "If I could walk, I'd rape you, Fanny Adams. D'you hear me?"

"Perfectly."

"Well. What d'you say then?"

"I say you'd better hurry up and learn to walk, hadn't you?"

183

He half smiled. "Bitch. You're the carrot and I'm the donkey, is that it?"

"If the cap fits, wear it, Hawkins. I'm darn sure I'm no carrot."

He laughed reluctantly and opened Zeek for me. It was a long time since we'd crossed swords like that and I used to enjoy it. Now my heart ached because I was deliberately deceiving him.

It started to rain in earnest during dinner. Hawkins said nothing about going outside, and when he telephoned at eleven it was to say thickly, "I love you, Fanny Adams. Please imagine me by your side tonight."

If we'd gone to Clevedon, Aunt Nell would have let us bowl along the front without umbrellas and drink the rain. But we couldn't go to Clevedon because Mr. and Mrs. Hawkins had come.

15

 MID-SEPTEMBER and every-
thing ticked over as usual at Thornton Hall. Stella
and Penny both passed history and geography O levels. Casey and Beamish went out regularly. Granny
and Mr. Pope quarreled amiably. Mrs. Tirrell wept
in corners and treated her husband to the ice treat
ment every weekend. Bennie told me with oblique
glances that marriage was no happy-ever-after. Hawkins and I went to Clevedon twice and three times
a week; we swam together and spent hours in the
library reading; we took our chairs beyond the lake
and into the steep woods that led to the main road
and Hawkins made outrageous suggestions. I tried
to giggle. I tried to conjure up the smart-aleck replies
that had come so readily in the first weeks we had
known each other. I tried to act the way Juliet had

acted. But she was two years younger than me and had legs. And a family.

It was all wrong. Phoney. Off-key.

The little time I had borrowed from truth had stretched into three weeks, and every day it became more difficult to face Hawkins. To talk to him. To let him touch me and kiss me. And it became hourly more impossible to tell him why. Or to backpedal into the dull-and-heavy-as-lead routine.

And then, when I was thinking that I must make something happen; that I'd got to push a spoke into the supposed placidity of our lives to break the circle; then Granny and Mr. Pope disappeared.

It wasn't the sort of disappearance that causes hues and cries to be instituted—in fact at first it was absolutely unnoticeable. In fact—because of his funny digestion—Mr. Pope's remained unnoticeable. It was only Granny who was missed.

I said to Bennie the first night—listlessly and without a lot of interest, "Granny hasn't been in to any meals today. Anything wrong?" And Bennie said, "Not that I know of. Tired, I expect."

The next day I looked for Mr. Pope to ask him. He wasn't around.

I said to Hawkins, "What news of May?" in a Shakespearean voice.

"May? Who's May?"

"Granny. Second day she's missed lunch. And she's getting to like cole slaw under my expert tuition."

"Munching chocolate in her room, I expect. I didn't know her name was May."

186

"Maybe you weren't interested."

"You're snappy today."

"You didn't know her name was May. You didn't know she'd missed lunch. She's on the same damned floor as you—five doors away, to be exact."

"Okay. I'll visit her now. As my company here seems unwelcome."

He waited for me to beg him to stay. I surveyed the clumps of chrysanthemums bordering the lawn. They were so tall they had to be staked. Useless legs again. I said, "You do that, why don't you?"

He went across the lawn at about forty miles an hour and I slumped in my chair and felt relieved. Was it possible to feel relieved when Hawkins absented himself? It was. I could stop acting a part now only when I was in bed or in the bathroom.

He was gone all of five minutes.

"She didn't answer my knock," he said sulkily.

"Why didn't you go in? She never locks the door."

"And find her on the bedpan? She'd love that, I expect. Why don't you go calling, anyway?"

I didn't know why. After I'd spent the day downstairs (with Hawkins of course) I was so tired all I could do was get up the ramp and into the lift and run for Zeek like a scared cat. God, I wasn't going to have to *act* dull and heavy as lead. I already was. And he couldn't see it.

I said, "If Pope was around he'd know whether anything was wrong with her."

"You don't mean to tell me he's disappeared too? Well there you are then. There's your answer. They're

187

sacked up together somewhere having a high old time."

Unexpectedly I wanted to cry.

"You're obsessed with sex. You're spoiling everything."

He lifted a cruel eyebrow. "You mean there's something to spoil?" He looked at my face and said quickly, "Oh Fan. Sorry. Sorry Fan. Sorry. Kiss me. Just kiss me once and I'll be a good boy."

He jammed his wheels against mine, pushed his face forward, his mouth ridiculously pursed, his eyes closed. It was so *phoney*. I brushed his lips with mine and heard him give a gasp that sounded desperate. Then he grabbed me behind the neck with one of his powerful hands and shoved the other inside my T-shirt and under my breast so that it hurt. I pushed him off and hit out blindly.

"See?" My voice choked at him. "See what I mean? All you think of is sex!"

He eyed me narrowly, coldly. Then he said, "You know why Mrs. Tirrell is always sniveling? Because she's playing ducks and drakes with Beamish and her old man. She wants one of them to grab her hard and let her have it."

"And you think I'm like Mrs. Tirrell?" I panted.

"Do I?" He was as cool as a cucumber suddenly. It was me who was hot and shaking now. "Maybe I do. Yeah. Maybe that's it. You've got to suffer, so you're going to make damned sure everyone else does too. Yeah."

He turned his chair and went off across the lawn

and I watched him go. In a way it was a solution. A good clean quarrel, a good clean break. But Beamish was right twice over about this whole thing. Luke Hawkins knew how to hurt.

That lawn was big and hard to cross on your own. As I said, I hadn't been on my own much for weeks now. Unless I was in bed or in the bathroom. Maybe I'd better get used to it.

I couldn't find out a thing about Granny.

Bennie said, "She's not too well, I think, dear. Keeping to her room for a couple of days."

The dinner helper said, "Yes, I've taken her a tray. She hardly touched a thing."

Immediately after dinner, Hawkins shot back to his room, so I forced my lethargic chair along to number eleven and knocked. No answer. I opened it and looked inside. The bed was stripped, nothing. I was in a panic. I nearly knocked on number five and then didn't. When Bennie arrived to tuck me in I asked her straight out if Granny was dead.

"Don't be silly, Fran. Of course not. Her arthritis is painful and she wants to be by herself. That's all."

"Don't give me that, Bennie. She's not in her room. I've looked."

"She was moved. At her own request."

"Where?"

"Fran, stop nagging. She was moved so that she couldn't have people dropping in. That's the way she wants it."

"But we're *friends*."

"And she knows she can get you on the phone when she wants you, dear."

At eleven forty-five P.M. the phone burped. And again. And again. I watched it and finally picked it up because I knew if I didn't he'd be hammering on Zeek in another ten minutes.

He didn't ask why the delay. He didn't apologize or say, "Aw come on, Fran." He spoke in a brightly conversational voice.

"I've had a long chat with Mrs. Tirrell. I thought you might be interested to know that a woman who wants kids and can't have 'em gets pretty mixed up at times."

I said, "Granny's moved rooms. I can't get hold of her."

He said, "There you are. She and old Pope are sacked up together—"

I put the phone down. He didn't ring back.

The morning dawned late and heavy with cloud. It was Sunday. We were supposed to be seeing Hawkins' parents; he thought his father had got the ramp done by the patio steps, and he was hoping they'd take us to his place to see it. I'd never seen his home. He was convinced that one glimpse and all my doubts would disappear. I stayed in bed and looked at my dormer and hoped it would rain so that I'd have a good excuse for not going.

Casey knocked and came in. She was disappointed

I was still in bed but didn't say so as she would have done at one time. I wondered if that meant anything. We started on the routine. By the time I'd had my bath I felt a tiny bit more with it.

"What's wrong with Granny Gorman?" I asked, watching her from the corner of my eye as I toweled myself.

"Legs. Arthritis. Bit depressed."

I frowned. It was all too pat. Something didn't add up. I tried another angle.

"What about Mr. Pope?"

Her eyes came up in surprise. "Didn't you know? He left—a couple of days ago."

"Left?" This was it. "He couldn't have. He didn't say good-bye."

"No?" Casey was as calmly casual as if we were discussing the weather. "He was disappointed because we couldn't help him more, I think. Perhaps he couldn't wait to shake the dust—"

"Casey. Tell me the truth. He's dead, isn't he? And Granny's taken it badly. She's shut herself up in another room."

Casey bustled around me, clipping my bra, then diving down to wriggle socks onto my feet.

"Don't be ridiculous, Fran. How you adore to dramatize everything." She looked up at me and her blue eyes were clear. "It's a storm in a teacup. They had a row and he left. Perhaps one day Granny will tell you about it. Until then—just leave it."

"Honestly?"

"Honestly."

191

"It all seems so funny and so unlike Granny. And unlike Pope too. He quite fancied her, you know. You haven't put her in quarantine because he had some frightful disease?"

"Fran, one of these days I'll murder you."

"If you'd give me her room number I'd know you were telling the truth."

She sat on the edge of the bath with a sigh.

"There was a fuss and Granny hated it. She only likes the kind of fusses *she* makes. Same as you. It was a fuss about nothing, Fran—and if you go ferreting her out and pestering her, you'll make it seem worse. Just let her alone to think about it all and she'll be all right."

"Okay, okay, I've got *some* tact, you know."

"Not much, if I remember correctly."

I let her have the last word. If Pope and Gran had had such a row that he'd left, I knew it was my fault for shoving them together in the first place. And I couldn't take much more responsibility.

She draped my dressing gown over my shoulders and opened the bathroom door for me. Outside, in his chair, Hawkins waited.

Casey said crisply, "I think we need some privacy, Luke. Off you go. Fran will see you at breakfast in fifteen minutes."

He ignored her.

"Fanny, are you all right? I had a ghastly dream. Are you all right?"

I pushed my chair slowly into the corridor. "You can see I am." I sounded heavy and dull as lead. For a ghastly instant I wondered whether Beamish had deliberately altered my drugs.

Casey said, "Go on, Luke. She isn't even dressed."

He bowled along parallel with me. Zeek stood wide and in my room all was chaos. I was ashamed because I'd stayed in bed so long and let everything go.

He said quickly, "Fanny, let's go outside before my parents come. Let's go down to the lake and see if we can spot those ducks again."

I said, "I can't. I'm going to chapel this morning." We had a beautiful chapel, sort of round and Byzantine, and I'd been there exactly twice in my whole four months at Thornton Hall and then only for Aunt Nell's sake. Now, it was sanctuary.

"Chapel? You never go to chapel." He half blocked Zeek so that I couldn't get in. His eyes were wide and astonished and then narrowed and hurt. "Fanny—you can't. It's a waste of time. It's a gorgeous morning for ducks, still and quiet. You can't go to chapel."

"Yes I can."

Casey snapped, "Luke, get out of the way. Now."

He backed off unwillingly. As I went past him he said tensely, "Fanny, if you're not by the lake at ten fifteen, I'll know. I'll know—"

Casey snapped harder, "Stop your blackmailing, Luke. Go down to breakfast."

I didn't look around at him. Maybe once he'd accepted the break it wouldn't hurt so much.

Casey stripped my bed and bundled soiled linen into the basket and said briskly, "He's had a bad night,

Fran. He'll be waiting for you outside the chapel. You'll see."

I was surprised how many of us were in chapel that morning. Stella and Penny—that was to be expected, they were the original conformists. Rosie and Dennis were there too, but probably they weren't given a lot of choice. Mrs. Tirrell never went—her husband always collected her early on Sunday and took her off for the day; yet she sat quietly thumbing her prayer book and trying to look brave. Henry and Mrs. Jarrett, who usually sat in the lounge or on the terrace reading the Sunday papers until lunchtime, followed me in. The staff were there in force too. Casey and Beamish sat together with wonderful naturalness and gave me my first chance of looking at them as a unit and seeing how right I had been. Not that I could be smug about it anymore, as I was making such a hash of everything else, but it was nice something was turning out right. Bennie, looking tired and drawn after her night duty, was there, and a girl was with her, maybe her daughter. I remembered Bennie was on her second husband, so presumably her daughter had a stepfather. Was that why she was here? Was it her way of getting half an hour of her mother to herself?

We sat there quietly under the domed roof, with its stained-glass outlets studded around the top and its gallery sweeping a midway circumference to descend to the floor in a fanning staircase that made every visitor exclaim with delight. We sat and waited for our visiting vicar, who fitted us in between his eight-o'clock communion and eleven-o'clock matins, smelled of sacramental wine and intoned—even his sermon. There was a coolness about the morning that made us shiver sharply at times in our still-summery clothes. Mrs. Tirrell rubbed the backs of her hands. Dennis fidgeted. Rosie lay in her converted pram and stared at the colored patterns above her, dreamily. Stella and Penny kept their eyes down reverently and probably thought about the A level courses they were starting that week. Casey and Beamish smiled at each other.

The vicar arrived and announced the first hymn. He held the edge of the pulpit and mouthed the words as he got his breath back. We sang vigorously; we all loved singing. Then we prayed for the Queen and all who govern with her, then we sang another hymn while the vicar kneeled by himself and prepared for his sermon. He stood up. There was a hush. He began. "Let the words of my mouth, and the meditation of my heart, be alway acceptable in thy sight. . . ."We all switched off and thought our own thoughts. I wondered whether Hawkins would be waiting for me outside. I no longer knew whether I wanted him to be there or not. I cogitated telling Casey everything and getting her advice. She'd be able to give it. Aunt Nell would cry. I'd have to keep it from Aunt Nell as long as I possibly could. Protect her as I was vainly trying to protect Hawkins. It came to me with a shock how much I loved Aunt Nell.

It was Rosie who first noticed that someone was in the gallery. I suppose because she was lying down

195

and her eyes were always looking up. Anyway she reached over and tugged at my cardigan sleeve and swiveled her eyes up and around. I looked.

At first I thought what she was thinking and my hand grabbed hers hard. A thin sepulchral figure, clad in white, a grayish halo outlining a minuscule face, had emerged from a doorway at the back of the gallery and was gliding to a vantage point above the vicar. And then I saw that this was no ghost. It was someone in a long off-white flannel nightgown, gray hair straggling over ears and neck and almost obscuring a very human face. It was Granny Gorman.

The vicar went on droning.

Granny seemed to pause in some task or other. She was lifting something. A bucket? It couldn't be a bucket. It was a bucket.

The vicar moaned about perfect love. It was very hard to associate love with the vicar. Rosie and I watched, fascinated. Casey had also spotted the figure. An electric tension spread from one to another of us. One coherent thought popped into the startlement of my mind and that was—the open door led to Gran's present room. This was her hideout. And she hadn't wanted me to find her, because there was no lift in the chapel.

The bucket was heavy. She heaved it along until she was above that oblivious intoning figure. Then she screeched at the top of her voice: "Can't a body get a bit of bloody peace even on a Sunday?"

It was shocking and terrible, that sudden furious voice splitting the hypnotic atmosphere of the chapel.

196

Like a knife plunging into a drowsy body, it was physical. Yet nobody moved. We all sat on, staring up at her with horrified fascination.

The vicar literally jumped. His whole body rose in the pulpit, his neck audibly snapped back, his surplice billowed around him as he stared upward. And then, odder and odder, he jerked his head back and went on with his sermon. He actually pretended Granny wasn't there and nothing had happened. A small flush colored his pasty face. Otherwise, no reaction.

He said, "Perfect love is perfect understanding. Where there is understanding, there is no need of forgiveness."

Granny screeched again. "Are you going to shut up or aren't you?"

"It is for Our Lord to forgive. Our human frailty precludes—"

Granny bawled, "I'll give you one more chance! Just one!"

We stared. Beamish stood up and Casey pulled him down and got up herself and began very quietly to climb the beautiful staircase opposite the altar. She took two steps at a time.

The vicar said, "Yet our Lord can be angry. We hear a great deal about the wrath of God."

"Right!" Granny leaned down and heaved the bucket onto the rail. Casey sprinted along the gallery. "Right—you asked for it! I'll show you about the wrath of God. Coming here and prating away right under my room!"

197

Beamish was halfway up the stairs. Casey threw out an arm in protest and gasped, "Don't—" And the bucket tilted and emptied its contents over the vicar's head.

As far as we could see, it was plain, clear water. Rosie couldn't stifle her giggles now, and Dennis had a hand over his mouth and rolled his eyes in an ecstasy of relief at the release of the tension of the last five minutes. Penny and Stella were turned to stone. The rest of us looked around, looked up, were lost between concern and our complete inability to do anything about it. The vicar spluttered and lifted his robes to wipe his face and dripping hair. Above him Casey and Beamish had Granny by either arm, and their voices made a soothing background to her continuing outraged protests. They persuaded her along to her room, through the door, closed it. And left behind silence and intense embarrassment.

Then the oddest thing of all. Just as Bennie was whispering to her daughter and about to move into the aisle, the vicar finished his emergency drying and pushed his cassock and surplice into place. Then standing there like a drowned rat, he said, "We hear a great deal about the wrath of God. Also about His powers of forgiveness. Which may seem anomalous. Perhaps the only conclusion we can draw is that God's anger descends on those who are unable to forgive. Who do not give others the opportunity to understand. Who withhold their trust and confidence in the name of pride. Stubbornness. Shame. Fear. And simply a lack of love." He did not meet our concerted gaze. He bowed his head. "In the name of farsonholy-gho—" He looked up. "We will sing hymn number five two nought."

We sang "Love divine, all loves excelling" in a kind of daze. Our thoughts chased around the chapel dome almost visibly. Had Granny flipped her lid and why? Was this what awaited all of us after so many years of instituted life? And what did the vicar *mean* when he just stood there and took what was coming and went on prosing? Was he ignoring Gran?

The hymn ended. The organist pumped audibly at the harmonium pedals while playing a thin note for the vicar's exit. He was short and fat, and purple with suppressed outrage. He couldn't wait to join the vicar in the vestry and say how disgraceful it was that in a home for the handicapped this sort of thing could be permitted to happen. Would the vicar agree? Or disagree? Or tell him to shut up?

The rest of us would have lingered, but Bennie and the other staff weren't having any. They pushed us single file into the cold tiled hall and at last to our own wide oak boards and the clatter of Sunday lunch being laid in the dining room. Released, everyone made for the lounge. I waited.

Hawkins was nowhere in sight. His absence might have been the reason for the dull gripes of nausea in my stomach. Or they could have been caused by Gran's demented outburst and my part in it. Anyway I waited, because Casey and Beamish had to come this way. And after a long ten minutes Beamish came alone.

He said, "Fran—"

I babbled, "Please let me see Gran. My second night here she told me I was beautiful and even if she says she doesn't want to see me—"

"She wants to see you." He smiled slightly. "She sent me to take you up. Let's go."

He hoisted me easily into his arms and I didn't even think about my wet rear beneath his hand. I held on around his neck and looked at my legs dangling uselessly over the crook of his elbow and thought how stupid and vain I'd been imagining for one moment they could be a mermaid's tail.

Beamish said, "Relax, Fran. She's quite calm now. She wants to get back to how things were. She thinks you can help her there."

We went back along the dark stone passage and into the chapel, across its tessellated tiled diameter and up the wide fanning steps to the gallery, along that felt-carpeted floor, past the discarded bucket and into Gran's new room.

She and Casey sat opposite each other on either side of the wide window overlooking the river valley and the motorway bridge. Casey seemed to be pointing out various landmarks. She jumped up as the door opened, and Beamish put me in her chair and immediately turned and left. Casey stood, hovering between us.

Granny said, "I'm glad to see you, Miss Termagant. I asked them to bring you up. You're the one for the news. I want to hear all the news."

I stared at her. I knew what she wanted. She wanted

the Fran of last June. The Fran who could say, "Got any more buckets around? Because if so I'll just fetch my umbrella." But that Fran was no more. So I stared at her and my eyes slowly filled with tears and I said at last, hoarsely, "Gran. Gran, what happened?"

She stared back. Then she drew her pugnacious chin right in and it quivered like a child's.

"What have I done, Fran?" Her whisper was a lisp of despair. "What *have* I done?" She looked at me as if she could see herself, and then she put her arthritic fingers over her face and keened loudly, rocking back and forth.

I reached for her, and Casey leaped to my chair and pushed me almost into her lap. I put my arms around the hunched shoulders and the straggly hair fanned over my wrists. I dragged her against me. Suddenly she let me take the weight of her. Her keening became interspersed with racking sobs.

I looked up at Casey through my tears and nodded and she touched me on the shoulder and crept to the door and was gone. I held Gran tightly.

"It's all right . . . all right. . . ."

Her shoulder bones were sharp and brittle in my hands. I could feel the misshapenness of her skeleton and it was as if kinesthetically I explored her life in those few racking seconds. And the funniest thing happened. First I felt a shaft of gratitude like light; it went through the absolute center of my body from the top of my head and even illumined my legs and feet. I knew with calm certainty that it was a privilege to die young. The knowledge came and went so quickly that I cannot recall it, but the gratitude remained. It was nothing to do with Gran's arthritic frame—nothing to do with escaping old age. Something to do with a journey; a journey toward something pretty good. And I would get there early. Yet it wasn't that either. It was shining and very simple and then was gone. The gratitude was a remembered glow.

Straight after that came another certainty. I had to tell Hawkins about my heart and lungs. I had to give him the chance to understand. That was what the vicar had been on about. I had to give Hawkins the opportunity to understand. Otherwise I would be like Mrs. Tirrell. Mrs. Tirrell . . . who hugged her ill luck to her and would not let Eric Tirrell share it.

So I held on to Granny's shoulders and waited for her to stop crying and share her pain with me.

16

 AT LAST SHE DRIED OUT. She
sat up, wiping her nose with the back of her hand,
and looked out the window, seeing nothing. I waited,
leaning back slightly and holding her hand. At last
she spoke, her voice muffled and thick with her crying.

"I've done something bad, Fran. It was a joke. Like
one of our jokes. And it turned bad on me. Really
bad. Cruel. I'm a cruel old woman. That's what I
am."

"Only with people who can take it, Gran. And that's
not cruel." I rubbed at the back of her hand and
then stopped in case the shiny skin sloughed off. "He
didn't mind, Gran. He thought he might be helping
you—letting you get something out of your system—"

"What you on about, girl?"

"The vicar. The bucket—"

"Oh that. I don't mean that—that's nothing. If they think I've gone mad and they send me away, then it's no more than I deserve. A just punishment."

"They're not going to send you away for emptying your slops over the vicar. You'll be famous for that. A heroine."

" 'Tweren't slops!" she flashed indignantly. " 'Twere good clean water from the bathroom. Took me ages to get it out without dripping it all over the floor." A touch of her old humor came to her voice. "I bet it was bloody cold, mind you."

"I bet it was."

I waited and she went back to looking out the window.

"No. It were worse than that, Fran. The vicar . . . he's paid to be humbled, isn't he? It's his job and it won't hurt him to be reminded of it now and then. But I chose someone who couldn't take it. One of us."

"Mr. Pope?"

"Arthur Pope." She sighed and her breath caught with sobs like cloth on a ragged nail. "I hope he gets to hear how I made a fool of myself this morning. It might make him feel a bit better. Just a bit."

I was silent, quite unable to guess what she could have done to cause such uncharacteristic regret. She stared and then she started up again.

"It was seeing you and young Luke. Gave me ideas, I suppose. Made me think I was still May Gorman who could be cheeky and get away with murder because of her bright eyes. Like you do, my flower. I wanted—" She took another retching breath. "I wanted one more fling. Before I gave up. A bit of fun. No harm to anyone. What they call these days a giggle."

She stopped as a piece of her gray hair sucked into the vacuum of her mouth. With my free hand I pushed it away and smoothed back the other wisps. She shook her head away from me.

"Leave it. I don't care anymore. Leave it." She moved her shoulders inside her nightie. "I haven't dressed since he went. I haven't bothered. I kept pestering them till they moved me up here so that no one could come calling. I can't eat. I can't sleep."

"You'll eat and sleep now, Gran. Just think of the vicar and you'll eat and sleep better than you've done for ages."

She turned her head and looked at me like a tortoise.

"I just hope Arthur hears about it, Fran," she repeated. "That's all. If I thought he could hear about it, it might be worth it."

"I'll make sure he finds out."

Sharpness returned to her face. "Miss Clever Clogs. How can you do that, pray?"

"Luke's parents know everyone. They'll find out where he's gone and they'll visit him and tell him. I promise you."

"A-a-ah." She exhaled another sigh and her lips pushed out pneumatically. "It would make it better for him, I reckon. Knowing. Knowing he was right in

205

the first place. Knowing I'm just a dotty old woman."

I said strongly, "You know as well as I do you're not dotty. Dotty people do dotty things without a reason. There's always a reason behind your dottiness."

"Oh yes. Vanity. I was forgetting." She thought back, doing some hard remembering. But the agony had gone. A tiny smile touched her concave mouth. "You know, Fran, I haven't lost my touch. I remember in the playground eighty years ago I promised a boy he could see my knickers if I could have some of his trifle. And in the World War—and remember I was over forty then, my girl—I led a couple of French soldiers a pretty dance. And I couldn't speak their language!" She snorted a semblance of a laugh and then was serious. "But I should know better now. And Arthur was a gentleman."

A pause. I thought I heard a distant clattering. Gran shook her head.

"When they came in to give me my morning tea and found him in his pajamas, I thought it was a laugh. I couldn't *stop* laughing. Nurse Bennett's face was such a picture. Then the silly cow sort of gasped and called him a dirty old man. Him. Arthur Pope. He couldn't take it—you can understand that, Fran. He couldn't take it. He shriveled. He almost fell down."

I knew my face had stretched wide.

"Mr. Pope was in your room all night? With you?"

"That's what I been telling you, girl. Don't look like that—it wasn't difficult. I told him I was lonely and had these dreams and where was the harm in it and . . . oh all kinds of things I told him. When he fell asleep I could have waked him. *I* was awake all night. But I let him go on. I wanted them to find him there. I wanted them to think May Gorman still had it in her. I imagined the story going all around . . . what you would say . . . and Luke . . . and how Helen Tirrell would get that frozen look. . . . I didn't think about him. Or how he'd feel."

I pictured it. Bennie with the tea. Mr. Pope struggling with sleep. Where had he been? Actually in Gran's bed?

"They sent him away, Gran?"

"No. They wouldn't do that. Course not. It was him. He couldn't stand it. He didn't want to see Nurse Bennett—or any of us again. He knew it would get around and he couldn't bear it, Fran. He worked in a bank all his life, d'you see. He had to be respected."

She was silent again and so was I. Yes. I could see how it would affect Pope. Now. I wasn't too certain that I would have known before. People could go along with you just so far and no farther. Mrs. Tirrell for instance. Hawkins?

There was a tap at the door and Casey came in with coffee and sandwiches. She put the tray on the bed and, with her usual neat-fingered efficiency, drew up the bed table and laid it, poured out two cups of coffee, looked at me and Gran, went quietly out again. What had she called this business—a storm in a teacup? Dear Casey, reducing everything to manageable proportions. A storm in a teacup which Mr.

Pope had been unable to weather. I freed my hand at last and passed Gran one of the cups. She took it without seeming to realize what it was and drank it down in loud sips.

At long last I said very very quietly, "I should think he would be very well respected. At his age. You too, Gran."

She looked up, not connecting my words with her own. Then she stared. "You're crying! Oh lordie—" Her voice shook with a kind of panic. "Not you Fran—you're not disgusted with old Gran, are you? Oh don't turn against me, girl—it was a bit of fun. I had to try it. I just had to *try* it. That's all."

I couldn't stop now I'd started. I'd done more crying since I met Hawkins than in the whole of my life before. She got a filthy hanky out of her sleeve and dabbed at my face, clucking like a hen; and at last I pushed her away and forced myself to breathe properly until I could speak.

"I'm not disgusted, Gran." I tried to smile. "I ought to be laughing. It's the most marvelous thing that has happened in Thornton Hall since it was built in seventeen ninety-four. Except for one other thing." I put my hands to my eyes and knuckled vision back to them. "Can't you see? You should be proud. Old Pope should be proud. You've struck a blow for all handicapped people and all elderly arthritics." I hiccupped loudly. "Hawkins said you were sacked up together somewhere and he was right! He was right!" I howled like a dog howling at the moon.

Granny recovered sufficiently to sound snappish.

"If it's so marvelous and wonderful, why are you crying your eyes out?"

I took her hanky and blew my nose furiously. This time I felt the well of tears subside until a dead feeling spread across my chest. When I spoke my voice was flat.

"You wouldn't understand, I suppose. I cried because . . ." I looked up at her and saw that she was concentrating entirely on me, her own horror abated. "Oh Gran, I'm *envious*! I'm so envious of you. You had him in your room. . . . Oh Gran. Don't you see? Luke and I—Luke and I can never—never—" The rotten tears surged up again like a maverick oil spout, and Gran enfolded me to her hard old rib cage and rocked me back and forth, back and forth.

When this third attack was over, she settled me back in my chair and reached for the sandwiches.

"Come on, Miss. We're going to eat these. And sit a bit more. Then we're going down to sit a bit more in the lounge and wait for the visitors. And you're going off with your Lucas Hawkins and thank God for every minute and for what you've got." She bit hard into a sandwich and mangled it into a far corner of her mouth. "Because . . ." Her wicked eyes looked at me. "Because I'm sorry to disappoint you, Fran, but nothing happened when Arthur Pope spent the night in my room. Nothing at all. We talked about old times and his ulcer." She tried to purse her leathery lips. "Don't reckon he could have managed anything else. He was such a nit-picker. And you can't say that about your Lucas Hawkins."

209

She mangled on happily while I watched her and let it all sink in. Then I started to snuffle a laugh. And so did she. Our talk had solved nothing, but it felt as if it had. And laughter is very therapeutic. When Casey and Beamish arrived to take us down we were still at it. I put my arms around Beamish's neck and tried to tell him by the pressure of my fingers that I was sorry I had almost hated him for the past four weeks and that I was going to tell Hawkins the truth at last. Maybe he understood. And to understand is the closest we mere mortals can come to forgiveness.

17

 HAWKINS WAS waiting for me when Beamish carried me down and put me in my wheelchair. So was everyone else. They were agog when their eyes went past me to Granny, who came Zimmering down the passage with Casey in attendance. They clustered around her and escorted her to the lounge in triumph. She was going to be a heroine. In the doorway she stopped in a kind of bewilderment and looked back at me. I winked at her with the whole left side of my face and suddenly she grinned and turned back to her questioners. "What else was I to do? I'd moved my room on purpose to get some peace and quiet. And it's Sunday, after all!"

I looked at Hawkins. "Well?"

He shrugged. "The parents will be arriving at any

minute. We might as well go through the motions. Or do you want to lie down after all your exertions?"

"I want to talk to you."

"That makes a change."

Casey came hurrying back. "Are you all right, Fran?"

"Yes." I smiled wanly up at her. "Thanks for the lunch. She ate it."

"She told you?"

"Yes."

"It was nothing, Fran. Whatever she said, it was nothing. He could have stayed. He was a funny, inhibited man."

"Yes." I gave a preliminary push toward the games room. "People get like that when they live in institutions."

She stayed where she was, looking after us, and for the first time I felt her pity. It would have been no good asking her advice after all; there's nothing so interfering as pity.

We went automatically to the billiard table where we always seemed to meet with the Hawkinses. He was stern and unforgiving; I could feel his hardness bruising me.

I said again, "Luke. I have to talk to you."

"I heard you the first time. Anyway Penny and Stella already told me. Gran threw water over the vicar."

"No. Not that. I mean—yes, I have to tell you about that too because it affects us in a way. But it's something else." The lovely clarity I'd known in Gran's hideout was going; I felt confused and harried.

212

"Spit it out then. The parents will be here any minute."

"I don't mean now. We can't talk now. Can we meet after dinner?"

"I suppose so. Not the lake, we shall frighten the ducks. The aspen tree."

A while ago—in another lifetime—I might have said, "Bugger the ducks," and won an unwilling smile from that unrelenting face. Not now.

Somehow the day wore on. We went to see the Hawkinses' residence. Tasteful and very modern. When Luke had told me it overlooked the river I'd imagined the river was getatable. Not so. The house was on the Leighwoods side of the Avon Gorge and the river was a million miles below. It was all like an eagle's nest.

They were nice to me. The ramp had been made alongside the steps leading to the patio. My room was gorgeous and being redecorated. Mrs. Hawkins had some carpet samples for me to choose from. Luke's room was next door. Mr. Hawkins said jovially, "After the Great Day we can knock a door through, huh?" I told part of Gran's story during lunch and made it sound entirely funny. I also asked Mrs. Hawkins whether there was any way of finding out tactfully where Mr. Pope had gone.

"Of course, my dear. I play golf with Millie Adeane. She's in charge of Social Services in this area and they're sure to have been notified."

"Granny wants him to know what she did."

"What an exhibitionist." Mr. Hawkins smiled.

213

I thought of Granny and her desperation.

"Yes," I said.

Mrs. Hawkins helped me onto the loo.

"Is anything wrong, Fran?" She hovered by the door in an agony of embarrassment. "I mean . . . well, what I mean is . . . you and Luke don't seem quite . . . the same."

So Luke got his gift of empathy from his mother. I smiled, warming to her instantly.

"We're running a sort of cold war."

"Can I—can we—do anything?"

"No."

She fumbled for the door handle behind her back. "I'll leave you, shall I?"

I smiled again. "I'll shout when I need help. I'm okay. Honestly."

She said, "I've thought such a lot about Luke and you. I think he's right. It was all . . . meant." She had the door open and was edging through it. "This will be your home, Frances. When you come."

She closed the door and I dropped my head, closing my eyes tightly on that well of tears that seemed bottomless. Dammit all, why did she have to choose now—with me on the blasted loo—to tell me I'd been accepted into the family?

He was waiting in the depths of the aspen shadow. I don't know how I got my chair across the grass; the dew was heavy.

His voice said, "I can smell the winter. It's Michaelmas, and Guy Fawkes will be burned in just over a month. Then it'll be Christmas and the New Year. The year in which we'll be married."

He had seen me coming, and spoke from the darkness like a voice of prophecy.

I said prosaically, "God, I didn't know you were there. Why didn't you cough? Or come to meet me?"

He moved his chair slightly and there was a glint of metal.

"Because I knew you wouldn't dash into my arms like you did before. And I couldn't bear it." He started to move away from me. "Fanny, don't let's have our talk tonight. Let's go around the garden like we used to. See which flowers are left."

"I can't. I'm too tired. And something must be wrong with my wheels. I can hardly move them."

He shoved himself around violently and the steps of our chairs clashed. "Then let me hold you. Don't talk—please don't talk. I know what you're going to say and I won't listen." He found my hand already on my wheel to back away and pulled me toward him with a jerk that nearly pitched me onto the grass. We grappled awkwardly and he pinioned my head and shoulders to his chest. Above our labored breathing his voice panted desperately. "I wish to God I *could* rape you, Fanny! Seriously, I would—here and now! Maybe it's the only way to stop all this rationalizing crap you're trying to give me! I've heard it all from Mrs. Tirrell, so you needn't bother to give me your particular version. You're both the same and it's bloody boring—let me tell you that! She thinks her old man would be better off with someone else

215

too. Someone who could give him a rabble of kids into the bargain. So however he feels, he's sacrificed. Well, I'm not hot on being a sacrificial lamb, Fanny! Got that?" He kissed me frantically. When I fought for breath he lifted his head and gave me perhaps three seconds, then he kissed me again.

I stayed quite still within his arms.

He said levelly at last, "You know, Fanny, I could hate you. Quite easily."

"Yes." My voice was dull. "I believe you could. Maybe you will. We can't get married, Luke."

His hands loosened on me and I sat up with difficulty.

"And why is that, Fanny? No—let me tell you." He mimicked my voice cruelly. "You want me to save myself for someone who can procreate. Produce a lot of little Hawkinses. For posterity."

I tried to ignore him; to stick to the line I'd planned.

"I knew. When I was with Granny this morning. It came to me quite suddenly that I must tell you."

His voice rose incredulously. "Because it didn't work out for her and old Pope? You're trying to draw parallels between them and *us*?"

"Oh Hawkins. There was nothing like that. They just spent the night together. Time together. Alone. That was all."

"They couldn't make it, you mean? And that worried you too? Christ, Fan, isn't there something—just one small item—that you *don't* worry about? Listen kiddo, you're missing the point with Gran and Pope. Like you just said—they were *together*. You think I want more than that? Let me spend the night with you, Fan, and I won't try anything, I promise. I'll lie on your bed with you and hold you against me. Just be *with* me. Like it was at first. *Please.*"

He was near tears; I couldn't bear that; I had to stop that at any cost.

"Hawkins, it was fun at first. Don't you see that? Everything was *fun.* Now it's not. Nothing is fun now—"

"Your fault, Fanny. Because you—"

"Yes. My fault, Hawkins. My fault. Because I can't go on. I can't . . . *continue* . . . *evolve.*" I put my hands out to fend him off. "Just listen to me, Hawkins! Can't you see I can't face us—you and me—developing into anything else? And it can't stand still—we can't stand still. That's impossible. So—so—"

He said angrily, "What the hell are you talking about? You're sixteen. I'm eighteen. Give it *time* for God's sake."

Thank God he was angry.

I said very calmly, "No. No, Hawkins. I can't give it time. That's something I haven't got. I should have told you sooner. I'm sorry."

I could hear him breathing but I couldn't see him. How kind darkness is.

He said at last, "You're trying to tell me you're going to die quite soon. Is that it?" His voice was cold as the November ocean.

"Yes. I was supposed to die at eleven. And I didn't. I'm five years in the red. But Beamish seems to think a year. Maybe two. I'm not so sure."

"I see." A long pause. "Everyone knew except me. Like the cuckolded husband."

I knew whatever I said now would drive him mad. I sat there and waited. He began to wheel himself across the lawn. I've never seen a drunk in a wheelchair, but I imagine he'd look like Hawkins did then. I pushed myself after him.

He accelerated and put his chin on his shoulder.

"Leave me alone. Just leave me alone will you? I've got to think—"

"Hawkins. I'm sorry."

"Yes. Yes, I expect you are. It must be rotten for you. Never mind. You've had your *fun.* That was what you wanted wasn't it . . . your *fun?* Maybe you've got enough time to have fun with someone else, Fanny. But not with me. For Christ's sake not with me!"

I let him go. I didn't move until I realized how much I was shivering. Then I bent to my wheels again. Out in the moonlight I could smell the frost. Winter was in sight just as Hawkins had said. At last I got off that thick sticky grass and over the gravel, along the terrace and into the blessed warmth of the house. Going up in the lift I thought he might phone me and I unlocked Zeek and bashed him open unceremoniously. But there were no burps that night. I didn't sleep all night long and there were no burps at all.

18

 THE NEXT DAY the dahlias
were all blackened and the chrysanthemums looked
as if they'd fall down if it weren't for Mr. Ottwell's
stakes. I watched him from my dormer as he went
around nipping the dead blooms into a big plastic
sack. He scorned secateurs. His horny thumbnail was
as efficient and much kinder. Later he went behind
the swimming pool, where he had a slow, perpetual
bonfire going. The cremation of the frosted dahlias
was a sweet-scented affair; I opened the window and
breathed it in with the sharp, cold, sun-filled Michaelmas air.

Casey came in with some milky drink.

"You missed physio," she accused. "Miss Hamlin
is furious."

219

I smiled, quite unable to find the energy to say the obvious—that Miss Hamlin was never furious.

Casey snapped, "Are you ill?"

"No."

"Not worried about Mrs. Gorman?"

"No." I'd forgotten Granny. Fleetingly I wondered whether she was back in her old room.

"Mr. and Mrs. Hawkins okay yesterday?"

"Fine."

"Then why are you here?"

"Tired."

"Not hiding?"

"No."

She put away a few things, stirred the drink, placed it on a little tray that clipped to my chair, clipped the tray into place.

"Thanks." We both knew that as soon as she left I would pour it away in the bathroom. If I could get to the bathroom.

She sat down on the bed. Casey the ever-busy sat down on the bed.

"I want you to be the first to know," she said belligerently. "Douglas and I. We're getting married."

I looked at her. White cap like a halo on golden hair; strawberries-and-cream complexion, cornflower-blue eyes, full—but firm—mouth. Very firm.

I clenched my hands to stop the tears. "When?" I asked hardily.

A glimmer of a smile twitched her eye corners.

"I forgot you'd want it all cut and dried. The actual date has not been fixed."

"Make it soon," I advised.

"Why?"

"Just do."

We stared at each other. At last she said, "Well. Thanks for the congratulations and best wishes. I knew you'd be pleased."

"Yes."

She stood up briskly. "I can't waste time like this. Drink your drink. I have to take the cup straight back down."

I nearly choked getting the glucosed milk down my throat. She stood by unrelentingly until every last little drop was gone.

"They're doing yesterday's chicken in a fricassee for lunch," she mentioned as she stood holding Zeek. "You like that."

"I don't think I want any lunch."

She tightened her mouth. "Just because Luke has gone home for the day you're pining."

I kept my face down until Zeek closed after her. Then at one o'clock I struggled down in the lift. She was right. He wasn't there. He'd run out on me. I sat by Gran and gave her my chicken and mashed my potato into the white sauce and swallowed two forkfuls. It was the best I could do, but no one noticed because Gran was still holding court. And it stopped anyone getting suspicious and putting two and two together.

The next day Mr. Ottwell started putting in the wallflowers for next spring. It was cold and clear and sunny again. He scooped out a little hole, parting the earth with his fingers, then he held the spinach-

221

green plant upright while he pressed the loose soil around it.

Hawkins wasn't at lunch again.

Granny said, "Where's that young man of yours, Miss Termagant? He wasn't around yesterday, was he?"

"He's gone home for a few days," I said, looking at my salad and wondering whether I could possibly manage to swallow a slice of cucumber. Or whether the tomato might slither down more easily.

Granny said, "Getting it all nice for you at their big house, so I hear? You'll soon be leaving all your old friends. Going off with your wealthy young man. Living it up, don't they call it?"

"Yes. Living it up."

"You'll forget all about us," she said lugubriously.

"I'll never forget you, Gran."

"Yes you will. Don't contradict me, girl. It's only right you should forget us." She watched me trying to skin my tomato. "I'll be glad when all this green stuff is over and done with. Nasty cold meals—they never satisfy a body. You look as if you could do with a few stews and puddings. All skin and bone you are. When's he coming back?"

I didn't ask who she meant.

"Not sure. When he's sorted things out."

"Then you'll leave."

It wasn't a question so I didn't reply. There was a silence, and when I looked up to ask if she could possibly manage my nasty cold salad her turkey throat was gobbling all by itself.

I said, "What's up?"

She said, "I'm going along to my room for some chocolate and a rest."

"Aren't you well?" I tried to really look at her.

She snapped, "I'm perfectly all right, thank you, Miss Termagant. The company isn't up to much though. Is it?" She half rose and shot her head at me like an attacking snake.

"Sorry," I muttered stupidly.

She turned with much chair scraping and hung herself over her Zimmer. One of the helpers dashed forward and picked up her horrible hanky and her bag. She Zimmered two or three steps, then turned for her parting shot.

"I just hope I'm gone before you. That's all."

There was another sharp frost and it was the turn of the roses. Not all of them. Some, in the shelter of the protective box hedges, still bloomed fragilely. I wondered whether they wept for their burning companions. There was no need. It would be their turn soon.

Casey wheeled me down to physio against my will and Miss Hamlin slapped and pummeled me with even more energy than usual. When she rolled me over and pulled me up her face was bright red and her teeth bared.

"Any more sensation, Fran?" she panted.

I shook my head. "I don't know why you bother. You're wasting your time."

She looked at me, her face wide open.

223

"What?" She rocked back on her heels and lifted her ribs for a gigantic breath. "I've heard my job called a lot of things—sometimes I'm a torturer—but I'm never a time waster. How dare you insult me like that, Fran!"

I shrugged and leaned down to haul up my jeans. She said, "You don't get out of it like that, Fran. Look at me."

I looked. Agate eyes, no depths to search.

"I suppose you're thinking of Rosie?"

Why should I think of Rosie Jimpson in her pram, smiling warmly at everyone as they coddled and petted her? And then I knew in a flash. I almost cried aloud with the pain of it. Rosie, in her protected spot, would survive a little longer than some of us. Only a little.

Miss Hamlin said very quietly, her breathing quite controlled, "If you think any time spent with Rosie is wasted then you're not seeing straight, Fran." She pulled socks over my feet and swung me into my chair. Her hand rested on my shoulder for a moment. A very strong hand, short fingered and spatulate with large knuckles and no ring marks. That afternoon I helped Rosie with yet another jigsaw puzzle. It was so boring she fell asleep in the middle of it as she always did. I didn't wheel away. When she woke up I'd started on the middle and left the straight edges for her. It didn't make me feel particularly good.

Beamish said, "So you told him?"
"Yes."

"Just like that. Straight out."

"Was there any other way?"

"I should have thought so. You could have admitted you were scared. Asked for his help."

"I'm not scared, Douglas. I am *not* scared."

"Then you're more of a fool than I imagined possible."

"Look. It was you who foretold all this. So let's just leave it. You're right. Leave it at that."

Pause. Another heartlessly sunny day. Mr. Tirrell wheeling Mrs. Tirrell toward their car parked to the left of Beamish's window. Was it Sunday then? What had happened to the rest of the week? Where was Hawkins? And where—oh where—was Aunt Nell? I had lived for Sunday and Aunt Nell and it was here and she wasn't.

Beamish came and sat on the window ledge in my line of vision.

"You make me sound God-awful. Am I really such a sententious, smug slob?"

Nice bit of alliteration that. Dylan Thomas liked alliteration. I had come across "Bible-black" last night. Was death Bible-black?

I said, "You need Casey. I don't know what sententious means, but you need Casey."

"I know." His hand touched mine. "Thanks, Fran."

I tried to smile. "Anytime."

He said violently, "God. Why didn't you ask Luke for *help*? Why do you always have to be so strong?"

"That's the way it was." Mr. Tirrell lifted his wife into their car with great tenderness. He left his arms

225

around her and kissed her cheek. She sat like a statue. "If I'd drooped all over him it would have been . . . different. We weren't like that, Douglas." I tried to find words to explain our curious relationship. "We were sort of abrasive. I didn't want Luke to turn into a nurse."

He said, "I'm going to go and talk to him."

"No!!" I flung off his hand, jerked my chair so that I was absolutely square to him and screamed the single word in his face. "No! No! No! Do you hear me, Beamish? If you do that you will spoil everything—every last damned thing. Can't you understand? Hawkins and I had something special—we were already losing it when I told him. So we cut it off clean. We've still got that—we can look at it and remember it. And if you bring him back here to patch things up into some second-rate, second-hand—" I was blubbering snot. I wanted to claw his face.

"Okay, okay." As before he held my jabbering hands in his and absorbed their violence. "I won't do it, Fran. I won't do it—just take it easy."

After a bit I took it easy. He let go my hands and sat back on the window ledge. I looked past him and saw that the Tirrells' car had gone.

I said quietly, "Is it Sunday?"

"Yes."

"Where's Aunt Nell? Where are the Parrishes?"

"She thought you and Luke would be going to Leighwoods."

"That was last Sunday."

He got off the window ledge and fiddled with something on his desk. "Obviously she thought that you and Luke and his parents would wish to spend a lot of time together."

A knot that had been in my stomach since last Sunday night tightened with a jerk.

"You've been in touch with her?"

"She rang through. Yes."

"When?"

"Yesterday as a matter of fact." He turned, smiling. "As she isn't coming today we thought—Linda and I—that *we* might take you out somewhere."

"Linda?" Was this another dream?

"Casey."

"Is that her name?" I looked to the window again, knowing it was a dream and that the Parrishes' station wagon would be rolling up the drive to rescue me from it. The drive was empty. I said, "If she rang yesterday why didn't you tell her about . . . about Luke and me?"

"I thought you should tell her yourself."

"How can I when she isn't coming?" The knot was so tight it was strangling something inside. "Listen. Beamish. Is she ill? What's happened?"

"No, she's not ill. I think . . . she wants to be by herself for a little while, Fran. She's like you in that."

Pain was everywhere. I said wildly, "Are you trying to tell me she and Uncle Roger want to give me up?"

He picked up the phone from his desk and dialed a six-figure number. Clevedon had six figures. We waited tensely. Then he said, "Mrs. Parrish? Doctor Beamish here. Can you hold the line a minute—I'm not certain whether Fran wishes to speak to you or not."

He put his hand over the receiver.

"She doesn't want to give you up, Fran. Do you want to ask her to come out here and fetch you?"

I swallowed convulsively. The habit of years dies hard even at sixteen. I shook my head stubbornly. If she didn't want to come I could manage. I'd managed so far.

He said steadily, "I'm not sure whether I should tell you. She asked me not to. But I will anyway. Roger has left her. He's played around for years but always stayed with Nell. Now he's gone. With his secretary. Nell's alone."

The knot started to loosen and the tears came. I reached for the phone. And then I could hardly speak. I managed something like, "Aunt Nell. I need you. Luke has gone and I need you. Please come and fetch me as soon as you can."

She didn't say anything for about three seconds. Then she whispered, "I'll be with you in half an hour, Frances dear. Ask Casey to pack an overnight bag." And she put down the phone. How could I have thought for one solitary instant that Aunt Nell would chicken out on holding my hand?

I stared at Beamish.

"I'm sorry. I can smell my pants. I must have wetted myself."

So Nell and I were together for the next three days and we comforted each other. We behaved very normally. At eight o'clock she would run my bath and

228

help me into it. Then she'd hover and try to help me while I slapped her hand away and gasped, "I'm perfectly capable. . . ." And then we'd have breakfast in the window overlooking the front; that would last a long time because although it was the off season, the sunshine brought a lot of retired people from Bristol to stroll along and look at the Channel and talk about the Indian summer. Then we'd wash up and plan lunch and go out to buy it. Sometimes we had fish and chips in newspaper and ate them on the slipway and then drowsed half the afternoon away against the warm stone. Aunt Nell wanted it to go on always. She said, "Fran. You can see we're managing. Why can't it last?"

"Because." I smiled at her in case she was hurt.

"Because why?"

"Because I need to have somewhere to run to. This is the perfect place. If I have you all the time—"

"That's nonsense, Frances dear. And you know it."

I smiled again and closed my eyes. I felt her hand on my arm and I put my other hand over and covered hers.

Not once did we talk about Uncle Roger. Or Luke.

We had wintry teas in the window; muffins and jam and watercress sandwiches and Genoa cake and very hot strong tea with loads of sugar. It would get dark and we'd switch on the television and have the news and then we'd play cards or chess or read or talk about our favorite things.

I told her I wanted to go out in the rain.

"Then you shall." No arguments about catching pneumonia. "The very next time you're here when

229

it's raining, I'll come along the front with you."

"Without an umbrella?"

"Without an umbrella."

"No hat—no raincoat—just a shirt and jeans?"

"You're mad. But okay. For five minutes only. Then a hot bath and bed."

I'd really got her going now. I took a long shaky breath.

"There is one more thing. You'll never let me of course. But it would be the best thing ever."

She eyed me with suspicious blue eyes.

"Go on."

"I'd like to—adore to—swim in the Channel."

The blue eyes widened. "Out there? In that murky water out there?"

"I'm a pretty murky character myself. It would suit me. Oh Aunt Nell, it would be wonderful. I'd be a real mermaid—"

"Maybe next summer we could go down to Bude. The water is clean there and there's a lovely sandy beach."

"No good. Too nice. Too proper." I jerked a thumb backward. "This is my sea. And I don't want the summer and the crowds all gawking. I want to go in the rain. And when it's dark."

She looked at me and tried a joke. "You'd get awfully wet."

I laughed. "I'd be so excited I'd probably steam."

"But Frances dear. It's so muddy and all weedy. And you'd have to have someone with you."

"Yes. You. Don't you see—we could do it. If it

rained next weekend we could do it then. You and me. And think how we'd feel after! Like that bloke who climbed Everest. Like Amy Johnson in her little plane."

She went on looking and she didn't say no. She didn't say yes either, but I could see I'd planted the seed. I didn't say any more. Mentally I held my breath. And it gave me something to live for. Does that sound crazy? Well, that was me all right. Crazy. And Aunt Nell kept eyeing the sea speculatively. As long as I live I'll remember how she kept looking through the window.

At other times we talked about Casey and Beamish and how good that was. About Granny and her indomitableness. Even about Mrs. Tirrell and her determination to be a martyr.

Aunt Nell said fairly toughly, "Don't worry about her, Frances dear. She enjoys it."

"I won't," I promised. And then quite suddenly I decided to tell her. No reason. I simply couldn't keep such a secret from someone who was now part of me. "Hang on to yourself, Aunt Nell. I won't worry about Mrs. Tirrell. Or about anything else. Because. Because there isn't time."

She didn't understand.

"Why? How?"

"Hasn't Beamish ever given you a clue? I asked him not to and he's a good man . . . but . . ." I put my hand over hers. And told her.

She didn't argue or try to reassure me. I told her everything. How I'd heard a couple of nurses talking

231

when I was ten. How I'd been playing them up all day pretending I was a princess. How—because I was left on those damned steps—I used to pretend all the time I was someone famous. How I'd been ordering the nurses about and being unbearable and then how the one said to the other . . . Try to be patient— her heart's weak and she has respiratory difficulties . . . won't live more than a year or two. And how when I got to be fifteen I thought I'd scored over the nurses and God. How they offered me a place at Thornton Hall and I knew Thornton Hall was very expensive and the Social Services wouldn't pay for me to go there indefinitely. So how that first night I asked Beamish and he told me that diagnoses were proved wrong every day. Every minute of every day. So I knew then that there wasn't much time. And I asked about a heart transplant and he said maybe. Yes. That was a possibility. So I knew again that a heart transplant was out.

I told her how I knew this with one part of me— my head—my logic. But that there were other parts that wouldn't believe my head. Until Beamish warned me to go easy on Luke. And then . . . oh yes, right then . . . I knew with all of me.

Aunt Nell listened. It took me ages to say all this. Nearly an hour. She didn't interrupt once. I realized at the end that I was still holding her hand.

Still she was silent. I expected her at the very least to nag me to come and live with her. She didn't.

She sighed and released my hand and got up to switch on the light and pull the curtains.

Then at last she spoke.

"It's still not in the least cold, is it, Frances dear?"
she asked. "Next weekend, whether it rains or not,
we'll take that swim."

I said hoarsely, "Thanks, Aunt Nell."

Someone had oiled Zeek's hinges. And the cleaners
had been at my room. There wasn't a single flower
in it and the vases were washed and stacked along
the back of the table like blindfolded men awaiting
a firing squad.

I telephoned Beamish.

"I'm not dead yet. Have you got someone else lined
up for my room?"

He replaced his phone. Three minutes later he
knocked on Zeek and came in holding his side and
fighting for breath.

"Another crack like that, Fran, and I smack your
bottom above the sensation line!"

"Well look at it! I've only been away three days!"

He didn't look. He sat down and dropped his head
onto his hand and got over his sprint. It was quite
a way down to his room and he must have used the
stairs—he'd been too quick for the lift.

Meanwhile I wheeled myself around the room mum-
bling complaints like Granny Gorman.

At last he said, "Hey. You're better."

I rolled my eyes. "The great Doctor Beamish! Orthopedic Surgeon Extraordinaire. Psychologist Mag-
nifique."

He grinned anxiously.

I said, "Instead of threatening me all the time why
don't you tell Eric Tirrell to wallop Mrs. Tirrell. Black

233

her eye if necessary. Stick her in that fancy car of theirs, take her home and keep her there." Hawkins' words. Now it was too late I saw their truth.

He said mildly, "Okay."

I swallowed. Then asked what was for dinner that night. He frowned, obviously never noticing what food he ate.

"Something," he said vaguely.

It was a fairly satisfactory interview. When Mr. Ottwell knocked twenty minutes later with his arms full of chrysanthemums I thanked him and then said, "And thank Doctor Beamish too."

And then I was so darned tired I had to go to bed.

I suppose the realization that Luke had actually left Thornton Hall for good seeped into me gradually. I didn't ask and no one told me, but it was the middle of the second week he'd been away and there was no other explanation. I tried every way I knew how to get a look into number five but it was always shut when I went past. Once I even phoned; if he'd answered—if anyone had answered—I'd have clapped my receiver straight down. No one did. It was easier. Much easier without him around. He must realize that too. I tried to be grateful to him.

It was Saturday and Aunt Nell was coming. Casey said it was colder, so I wore a sweater and packed another one. I managed to sneak my bathing suit into my case without her seeing. There was fruit on the breakfast table and I ate a banana and swallowed it carefully. I wasn't worried about my lack of appetite. I would eat with Aunt Nell.

At ten o'clock she hadn't come. I went back upstairs and found Casey making my bed.

"I was going to do that," I lied. I hadn't done it since my last day with Hawkins. "I thought the cleaners were doing it anyway."

She went on working, flapping out a fresh sheet, slapping it under the mattress at the bottom, doing neat hospital corners.

"You don't like the cleaners coming in," she reminded me. "And anyway I had something for you."

"What?"

She nodded her head at Zeek's inside. I looked. An enormous willow grew up his middle and cascaded its fronds around my flowers.

"Hey!" I was openmouthed with admiration. "Casey! It's terrific! Where did you get it?"

"Wallpaper. Debenham's. Saw it last week and bought a roll yesterday. Thought it would fill in the top half."

"I kept meaning to ask Bennie to do it for me Casey, it's beautiful. Thanks."

"My pleasure." She picked up the laundry bag and made for the door. "Have a good weekend."

I wanted to tell her about the swim. I wanted to tell her much more than that. But she was gone.

At eleven I rang Beamish and asked him to phone Aunt Nell's number from his room. He rang back to say there was no answer so she must be on her way. I held Dorothy on my lap and looked at the

235

willow. Cricket bats are made of willow because it is so pliant and can absorb shocks. Weeping willow.

At twelve I stuffed Dorothy on top of my case and went downstairs to wait for Aunt Nell. No one was about. I went into the lounge and spoke to the dogs. They rolled on their backs and their tongues fell out of their open mouths onto the floor. A clatter of dishes came from the dining room; a desultory *tap-tap* of a Ping-Pong ball from the games room. I opened the French doors and pushed out onto the terrace. Clouds were massing up in the west and I wondered whether it would rain. Far down the ribbon of the drive, a car appeared driving very slowly; the station wagon. I waved fruitlessly and bowled my chair down the ramp and onto the lawn, weak with relief. I was behind the box hedge. I stopped and lifted myself on my arms to call again to Aunt Nell as she pulled up. Then I sat down again. Uncle Roger was driving the station wagon. And beside him, his leonine fair head as angry as ever, was Lucas Hawkins.

I did not know what to do. I cowered in my chair with my heart hitting my ribs and my stomach sick with fear. The car door slammed. Someone came out of the house; there were low voices. The rear doors squeaked and there were the usual clicking sounds of a chair being unfolded. Then wheels on the gravel. The front door shut.

I put my head on my stupid knees and wondered how I could get back to my room without being seen and lock Zeek and not answer the phone. I raised my head and the garden swam around and then flowed through me like a river. Frantically I jerked my wheels, got onto the lawn and made for the aspen tree as if she might be waiting for me there all the time. I could hear someone calling her name. "Nell! Nell!" My chair was beneath the umbrella of whispering leaves and it was my own voice calling. I tipped my head back as far as it would go and fought to exhale properly before I sucked in more air. Funny that: I wanted to faint; wanted to get out of an unbearable situation. Yet my body did the things it should do to stay conscious.

Uncle Roger walked across the lawn alone. He wore his gray flannels but no white shirt and jacket. A heavy knit sweater instead. His shoes weren't clean either.

He got to me and crouched by my chair.

"Hello Fran." He covered my hand with his. "Hello. Hello Fran."

I stared at him. The sound of the restless aspen leaves entered my ears and filled my brain with their murmuring. There was no wind. Yet there must be. I could hear the sea. The murky gray sea where tonight I would swim like a mermaid.

"Won't you speak to me, Fran?"

His eyes were gray but not like the sea. They were clear; you could see into them. They had fooled me with their clarity before. They were as clear as a lying child's.

"Fran. Whatever you think of me, I love you. Will you believe that? Just nod. Just tell me you believe that, my dear."

Nell. Nell was left on the steps. Because she was barren.

"I have to tell you, Fran. I have to tell you. There's

no way to make it easy, darling. Nell . . . Nell is gone, Fran. I'm sorry—oh God, Fran. She's drowned."

My voice said flatly, "I don't believe it."

He dropped his head. He was hanging on to me with both hands now and I could feel the despairing weight of him.

"You've got to accept it, Fran. It's no good. . . . Her body was found this morning on the beach."

"No."

He rested his forehead on the inside of his elbow and he was crying. He talked in short cutoff sentences. A picture emerged: I shut my eyes and fought against it, but it grew with each word he spoke. The police at the top of the slipway. On the front under the strings of dead fairy lights, an ambulance, its blue light flashing. People, curious people. Men in thigh-high fishermen's boots lifting her off the rocks and putting her on the stretcher.

"It wasn't her," my voice said harshly.

"Fran . . . I had to identify her. It was . . . Oh God, Fran . . . how could she have *done* it?"

I looked down at the sandy head, still hating it, but through the heavy blanket of my protest a thin point of incredulity stabbed. Surely he didn't think *that*?

I said rationally, "That's not true."

He didn't recognize the change. His voice repeated dully, "It's true. It's quite true, Fran. Sometime last night Nell walked down that slipway and kept right on walking."

"No!" my voice said sharply.

He didn't hear.

238

"It was my fault. I know that. She was unhappy because of me—don't think I'll ever be able to forget that. But to do something so appalling—so dreadful—"

"No."

But I was tempted. Tempted to let Uncle Roger carry the burden of guilt instead of me. It wasn't any more than he deserved, was it? He'd left Nell on the steps. Nell and me. Revenge for Nell. Revenge for me.

The aspen leaves whirled in my head but beyond them, somewhere, a bird sang.

"No," I repeated.

"She was cut, Fran. The rocks had knocked her about—"

"No!" My voice rose to a scream and he lifted his head and put his arms around me. I fought him off.

"Fran—I'm sorry. I shouldn't have said that. It's just . . . you and she were so close and I had to share it with someone—"

I said in a high falsetto, "She didn't kill herself! She didn't kill herself! Do you hear me?"

I listened to my words and wondered why I spoke them. The roaring of the aspen leaves was dying. Aunt Nell had loved him. She had loved him.

He said, "Darling Fran. You don't understand. You're a child—how could you understand?"

Mrs. Tirrell's words. I said, "I understand. You think she had nothing else to live for. Because you'd left her. Because she couldn't have children."

A puzzled look crossed his ravaged face. Then he shook his head.

"Fran, it wasn't like that. Things are never quite so simple as that. Nell must have told you that to protect me. It was so like her—"

"She told me nothing," I said abruptly.

He kept looking at me. He took a breath.

"Then I'll tell you. Nell knew I'd come back to her, Fran. She knew I couldn't live without her. She . . . she wasn't the one who could not have children." He flushed painfully but held my eyes.

I stared back at him. Everything seemed to be waiting.

I whispered, "You. You're . . . impotent."

It was a word I had read but never spoken. As it emerged into that waiting stillness it had an awfulness all of its own. Impotent. I remembered looking it up. "Wanting in physical, mental or intellectual powers." It described me. And Uncle Roger. Not Aunt Nell. Aunt Nell had been fully potent. She had had all her powers. And she had used them to protect . . . us.

He didn't speak. His flush deepened but he kept looking at me. I leaned back in the chair. The tiny wind that moved the aspen cooled some sweat on my face. I closed my eyes.

"It was nothing to do with you." Still I whispered. But my words were clear. "She had no wish to kill herself at all. She and I were going swimming tonight."

"What are you saying, Fran? You're not making sense."

"Surely you see? One of my crazy ideas. And I persuaded her to let me do it. She was going to come with me. So . . . last night . . . being Aunt Nell . . .

240

she had to try it first." I tightened my eyes. Aunt Nell. If only I hadn't had this last crazy notion. If only I'd kept my big mouth shut. If only . . .

He said, "She was wearing her bathing suit. I thought it was just Nell. Neat and tidy to the last."

I could see her. Folding her clothes neatly in her room. Steeling herself. Because she hadn't wanted to do it. Had those big shoulders been very much bruised? Had she been frightened? I didn't think I could take this.

Then I felt Uncle Roger's hands on my face. I opened my eyes. He was standing up and looking at me and his eyes were so clear I felt I could look into his soul.

"Listen, Fran." His voice was low and urgent. "Listen to me carefully. Try to imagine how thankful Nell must have been. When she knew . . . when she knew she wasn't going to make it. Remember what Nell was like. Her one thought must have been that she had saved you from drowning."

I stared up at him. He had come out of his own misery and touched mine. He knew. He understood. He hadn't fooled me at all . . . this was his gift. He understood.

I heard that bird singing again. And I knew why Aunt Nell loved Uncle Roger. And across the lawn Casey came running, her beautiful face stretched tight with anxiety.

"Fran—Fran—are you all right?"

Her cap was gone and her beautiful golden hair tumbled over my face as we held each other and wept.

241

19

 THEY TOLD ME—warned me?—that Luke was waiting for me on my corridor. Casey said, "D'you want to rest in my room for a while, Fran? Or shall I stay with you?"

I shook my head. "What will Uncle Roger do now?"

She said, "There's a lot he has to do. Don't think about it."

"He brought Luke here. Has Luke to go away with him?"

"No. Luke is back in his old room. Roger went there first to tell Luke, and Luke decided to come back to Thornton Hall."

I grinned crookedly. "To hold my hand."

She thought I was bitter. "What is wrong with that, Fran?" she asked straightly.

"Nothing. Nothing at all Casey."

The lift doors opened and he was sitting in his wheelchair outside Zeek. He stayed where he was. I went to him slowly.

I said, "She didn't drown herself, you know, Luke."

He watched me. His eyes were very stripy and looked smaller than I remembered. Had he been crying too?

"I didn't think she could have. Not Aunt Nell."

"She promised me we'd go swimming tonight. When it was dark. She was trying it out."

He got all the implications. He said steadily, "She was inclined to be quixotic, was Nell."

I made a noise in my throat. "Yes."

He said, "This would please her. A lot."

Another noise. Was it hiccups?

"What?"

"Us. Here. Together."

I said violently, "If you're trying to say that because she's drowned we've got to forgive and forget all that's happened—"

"Don't be so bloody stupid." He didn't sound angry at all. Calm and very certain. He smiled slightly. "I meant simply what I said. Whether she's alive or dead. It would please her to know that we are together again."

A wave of pure sadness swept from my waist upward.

"Oh Luke. We can't go back. Too much has happened. All that—it's over. We were children playing in the sun."

"How often did I tell you that, Fanny Adams?" His

smile was sweet now. "It was you who wanted to go back. It was I who said we had to go on. We're going on . . . there was a pause and now we're going on."

I shook my head. "There's no way, Luke."

He said, "Give me the key to Zeek, Fanny."

I fumbled in my tidy bag and handed the key over. I didn't want to see him sitting in my dormer again. But I couldn't send him away either.

He unlocked Zeek and pushed him wide. Then he swiveled his chair and faced me.

"Watch this, Fanny."

I watched.

He took the rug from his knees. He wore jeans, and at the ends of the jeans were black shoes. Slowly, smiling at me, he leaned down and pushed his left shoe over to his right and tucked the step of his chair out of the way. Then he knocked his left leg to the ground and followed it with his right. He sat up and placed his hands on the arms of his chair. And shoved. A grunt came from him and he stopped smiling. But he was up. Standing free of the chair. No sticks. No crutches. Just Hawkins.

He took two swinging, jerky steps toward me and leaned down.

"No!" I gasped. "No—Luke—you can't do it— you'll hurt yourself."

"Shut up, Fanny. Will you?"

His left arm was around my shoulders, his right lifting my useless knees. Our faces were close and I could see the sweat on his. He heaved mightily and I left my chair. Like a weight lifter he rested, his face contorted. I flung my arms around his neck trying to throw my own weight with that next gargantuan effort. A noise, half groan, half shout of triumph came from him. And we were up.

He rolled to the left, then to the right. He staggered and leaned against Zeek's jamb. I focused on the first flower I had stuck to the oak; a forget-me-not. And then Hawkins pushed himself upright again.

We crossed the threshold.

He put me on the bed with a rush, turned and fell down. We sat there for a moment breathing deeply. Then he lifted his legs one by one next to mine and rolled over so that we were facing each other. We were exhausted. At last he got his right arm beneath my head and pulled me against him. And so we stayed until the early October afternoon had finished and the darkness was complete.

Then we talked. We talked in disjointed whispers, stopping now and then to hang on to each other tightly with a kind of terror. There was so much to say, yet there was nothing. The two stark facts—that Aunt Nell was dead and that we were together again— were there. We were frightened to admit that they were connected. If Aunt Nell was alive, would we be together now? Luke held me so tightly I could barely breathe. He said fiercely, "I couldn't have stayed away much longer. I couldn't have." And I said, "I'd have asked you to come back. Tomorrow . . . next week . . . I'd have asked you."

But we would never know.

We couldn't begin to realize the Roger-Nell relationship. The giving and the taking. And the giving again.

Luke whispered, "When you rely on someone as much as he relied on Nell, perhaps you're bound to resent it."

I cupped his face, trying to see it in the darkness. "Is that why you left me, Luke?"

He said, "I don't know. I don't know, Fanny."

We talked about the easy way we had dabbled in the lives of the Thornton Hall inmates. Casey and Beamish, Granny and Mr. Pope. Even Mrs. Tirrell. Our lightness terrified us now. Our only hope seemed to be to cling together until the strength of our own love steadied and settled. So we clung together. And we slept.

Sometime during the night I awoke and looked wonderingly around my room. Someone had pushed my wheelchair to its place by the bed and Zeek was closed. Moonlight lit the weeping willow, nourished into resilient toughness by its own tears. I drew my head back and stared at Luke. He looked vulnerable in his sleep, and very young. I kissed him and his eyes opened.

"I think you should go now," I whispered. "They've bent all the rules in the book for us. Let's show we appreciate it."

Two weeks ago he would have said, "Damn the conventions and damn them." Now he kissed me in return and smiled and began the arduous task of sitting up.

I said, "I'm not turning you out, Luke."

His grin was wicked. "If I thought you were I wouldn't go. Can you hang on to my hand while I reach for the chair? I don't want to fall off the bed and bring Bennie rushing up."

I said, "I love you, Lucas Hawkins."

He turned. "I love you too, Fanny Adams."

"Is it going to be all right, Luke?"

"Yes."

"Don't lie. Not to me."

He said, "We've got now. That's all anyone's got, Fanny."

He turned away, picked up his left leg and put it carefully on the floor, then his right. I sat up beside him and we looked at each other and smiled inverted smiles. With an enormous effort he stood up and began his spasmodic walk to the door.

Ten minutes later the phone burped.

"Darling." His voice was steady as a rock. "I had a thought on the way down. I'll hold your hand this end. And you can bet your sweet life that Nell will be there to take it at the other end. She never copped out on anything in her life, did she?"

I whispered, "How did you know I was scared?"

He said, "Because I am too. Idiot."

20
Conclusion by Lucas Hawkins

FRANCES ADAMSON died on the ninth of December two years ago.

On the second day of that month, she handed me four school exercise books in which were scrawled and scribbled what goes before this. The words were for me and I have hugged them to me since then as the last of our precious secrets. Now I can share them. I can share Fanny. Maybe even let her go a little.

That night in the garden I believed her instantly. I could look back and see that her recovery from pneumonia had been a fluke, a wonderful preordained fluke so that we could know each other. I saw that the high spot of her will to live had been reached as we kissed on the Ferris wheel. After that, after her talk with Beamish, she had softly, slowly declined.

I didn't give up immediately. I went to see Beamish and shouted at him that she should be protected and that swimming and physio and swanning around in her chair all day were ridiculous and he was not fit to be a doctor. He kept himself very still, bowed his head, took what I handed out, then said, "If a miracle happens, Luke, it will happen. Meanwhile, don't you think Fran would prefer to live as fully as she can?"

So I flung out of the place. Like Fanny, I thought our roles would have to change. I thought what we had was over. Then, when Nell drowned, I knew that everything was only just beginning.

I see she gave no description of herself. She was dark with very fluffy hair that sprang out of her head and would never lie flat. Her eyes were brown and very large. It was true she could resemble a marmoset. Also a bird. She was very small and fragile, and along the backs of her beautiful hands and on her temples there was a tracery of fine blue veins. If her legs had "worked"—as she always put it—she would have been a dancer. As it was she enjoyed a curious kinship with objects and humans around her, and she was constantly "interpreting" them, much as a dancer "interprets" music and movement.

Her spirit and her sense of fun were limitless. Before she died, she insisted she wished to be buried next to Aunt Nell in the cemetery above the sea— wearing her mermaid's tail. She said it mischievously and quite without solemnity. We laughed about it. But it was arranged.

A week after she finished writing I took her to my

parents' home, and for a while she was happy to be cloistered there with me, to the exclusion of everything else. Then she recovered her old spirit: She wanted to go back to Thornton Hall and share her happiness. We went back. For two weeks.

She would want me to add that Mrs. Tirrell now lives at home with her husband. Mrs. Gorman died peacefully in her sleep, a grin on her face, her teeth elsewhere. Staff Nurse Casey married Doctor Douglas Beamish on what would have been Fran's seventeenth birthday. I attended. Penny Davis was successful in gaining two Advance level certificates and is going to Bristol University next year. Stella will miss her. Incredibly, she is learning to type.

I am working in the family business. I go to Thornton Hall every Sunday, not because I want to turn back the clock but because there are things I can do there. Rosie is still alive and has some of Fanny's happiness. Dennis is improving. One day he might walk. When it rains we go outside and tip our heads back and drink the rain. Roger Parrish visits too, very occasionally. He has married his secretary and finds it difficult to talk to me.

For six months of my life I knew Frances Adamson.

Hardly any time at all, yet a lifetime. Almost nothing. Yet everything. Sweet Fanny Adams. Sweet F.A.